The Billionaire's Reluctant Bride

Books by Elle E. Kay

Faith Writes Publishing

ENDLESS MOUNTAIN SERIES:
Shadowing Stella
Implicating Claudia
Chasing Sofie

THE LAWKEEPER SERIES:
Lawfully Held
A K-9 LAWKEEPER ROMANCE
Lawfully Defended
A S.W.A.T. LAWKEEPER ROMANCE
Lawfully Guarded
A BILLIONAIRE BODYGUARD LAWKEEPER ROMANCE

Lawfully Taken
A BOUNTY HUNTER LAWKEEPER ROMANCE
Lawfully Given
A CHRISTMAS LAWKEEPER ROMANCE
Lawfully Promised
A TEXAS RANGER LAWKEEPER ROMANCE
Lawfully Vindicated
A US MARSHAL LAWKEEPER ROMANCE

THE BLUSHING BRIDES SERIES:
The Billionaire's Reluctant Bride
The Bodyguard's Fake Bride

STANDALONE NOVELLAS:
Holly's Noel
Painting the Sunset Sky (coming soon)

The Billionaire's Reluctant Bride

ELLE E. KAY

FAITH WRITES PUBLISHING

Benton, Pennsylvania

Faith Writes Publishing
266 Saint Gabriels Rd
Benton, PA 17814

ISBN: 978-1-950240-04-3

I dedicate this book to my husband.
He keeps life interesting.

Prologue

24 August 2006
Fenwick Island, Delaware

The light rain mingled with her tears as Addison sat beside Zachary on the beach. She'd turned seventeen that day, but during her celebration her boyfriend, Ben, dumped her so he could hook-up with her younger sister, Parker.

"Try not to be sad. He didn't deserve you." Zach's shoulders rounded as he leaned closer and wiped away her tears.

"I can't believe he dumped me for my sister. How can I still love him?" The rain fizzled out as she cried, but the breeze off the sea brought on a shiver.

"He's not worth the heartache. Forget him. It's our birthday. Let's celebrate." She and Zach shared a birthday, and every year no matter what they did during the day, they spent the last hour before curfew together. They both lived in the rural town of Lake Bethel, Pennsylvania, but their mothers met while on vacation in Fenwick Island seventeen years earlier.

All this time later, their families still spent summer vacations in side-by-side beachfront rentals. Zach had been her best friend as long as she could remember.

She sniffled and lifted her head so she could meet his clear blue gaze through his wire-rimmed glasses. He tucked a strand of her dirty-blond hair behind her ear and pulled her closer, letting her cry on his shoulder. A few minutes passed before she pulled away and stared out at the dark waves crashing against the beach. "Do you think we'll spend all our birthdays miserable? What is this the third in a row we've trash-talked an ex?"

"Yeah. Last year it was Heather the two-timing loser and the year before it was Sven. He was a goon."

"I guess we both stink at picking dates."

"Yeah, we do. Maybe we're both destined to be alone forever."

"That would be dreadful." There was a slight tremor in her voice.

"Would it?" he asked tilting his head to the side.

She scrunched up her nose. "I'd hate being alone. I want to marry and have a houseful of kids."

"In that case, let's make a pact."

"What kind of pact?"

"If we're both still unattached on our twenty-ninth birthday, we'll get married."

"To each other?"

He leaned toward her, and his shaggy blond hair fell over one eye. "Yeah, to each other. Who else?"

"Deal." She gave him a shaky smile and reached out her hand to seal the deal. "I guess there is a benefit in having a guy for a best friend."

Chapter 1

Addison laughed as she typed her response to Zach's email.

Sure. Why not? Set the date. Order the flowers. I'll be there.

He always had a great sense of humor. It surprised her he remembered the teenage pact they'd made to bring it up all these years later. Picturing her friend's laughing blue eyes teasing her, she grinned. It would be fun to have him back in her life again, but now that Fractal Enterprises had gone public, and he was a successful giant on the social media scene, it was unlikely he'd be able to make time to hang out with an old friend.

His response came quickly.

Why don't we set the date for our birthday? It would be fitting, don't you agree? I'll pick you up first thing in the morning. August 23rd to fly you to location.

If he wanted to keep the joke going, she would play along.

Our birthday. Why didn't I think of that? I'll see you then.

When no further response came, she shook her head and got back to work, busying herself designing a plug-in for a client's website. After a few hours of staring at PHP, she needed a break, so she called her mother.

"Want to meet for lunch?"

"Sure. I have a customer, but I should be able to get away in twenty minutes. Meet me at the diner."

Her mother disconnected the call before she could reply.

Addison arrived at the diner a few minutes early and found a booth in the back. Thoughts of Zachary Williams swirled in her head. She wondered how they'd lost touch when they'd been such close friends. Then she remembered the kiss that ruined everything. If he hadn't given her that pity kiss, they would've remained friends, but she'd been unable to face him after that night.

Her mother arrived with her usual flair. She was dressed in a bold lime green skirt and wore a purple feather boa draped around her shoulders. "Why did you sit in the corner?"

She'd found a seat in the back so her mother wouldn't embarrass her but would not come out and say so. "It's quiet back here. It makes chatting easier."

"Oh." Her mother snapped her fingers at a waiter walking past. "Water with a slice of lemon and a spritz of lime, please."

Addison cleared her throat. "Mom, it's a diner. They don't do a spritz of lime."

"They don't unless you ask them."

Switching gears, she leaned across the table. "I received an interesting email today."

"Did you?"

"Zachary Williams emailed me about a teenage pact we'd made."

"What kind of pact?"

"A marriage pact."

Her mother sat up straighter, giving Addison her full attention. "Tell me more."

"When we were seventeen, we made an agreement that if we were both single on our 29th birthdays, we'd get married. It was just one of those silly things kids do. Since our birthday is coming up, he joked about it and emailed asking if we're still on." Addison giggled. "He's the same fun guy he was back then. I miss him."

"What makes you think he was kidding?" Her mother's keen brown eyes bore into her.

She shifted in her seat and lowered her gaze. "He had to be kidding. Nobody takes teenage pacts seriously."

"Maybe he does."

"I hope not. I played into it. Told him to get the flowers and arrange the wedding."

"You may have agreed to marry the wealthiest man in America."

"Mom, he's not marrying me. It was a joke."

"Are you sure?"

"Yes, I'm certain. I know Zach better than I know myself."

"Zachary has had a crush on you since fifth grade."

"Has not."

"Yes, he has." A Cheshire smile graced Mrs. Scott's face. "His mother and I talked about it all the time, but you barely noticed he was a boy."

"That's not true."

"Oh, but it is."

"Maybe when we were young, but I crushed on him hard senior year. It's probably why I agreed to the silly marriage pact idea in the first place."

5

"You're not getting any younger, Addison. Marrying Zach would mean you could start a family."

"He doesn't want to marry me, Mom. The man was kidding. It was a joke."

"If that's what you want to believe."

They finished their meal in silence and Addison hurried back to the office. It had to be a joke. There was no possible way he could be serious.

Zachary Williams stared out the window of the high rise. His posture was rigid as he listened to his cell phone play "Crazy Ex-Girlfriend." It was the ringtone his personal assistant set for Nikki. Nothing could be more appropriate. It was the fifth time she'd called this morning. He'd answered the first three times. The woman wouldn't take no for an answer.

It was her fault he'd emailed Addison. If the woman had a shred of decency, she'd give up and leave him alone. He flashed back to the moment he'd caught her cheating. He'd gone into the conference room for a meeting with his lawyer and there they were. They had absolutely no shame. It was clear what he'd walked in on. He'd walked away quietly and started the search for a new lawyer. Finding a new woman proved more difficult. He'd dated several women before Nikki, but she was the closest he'd come to tying the knot.

When it appeared he might not find a suitable girl in Los Angeles, he'd remembered the lovely brown-eyed girl back home who was his perfect match. Kind, funny, and genuine. That was when he'd reached out to Addison to see if she was interested in following through on their marriage pact. Thankfully, she'd agreed and his search for a wife ended.

When the phone stopped ringing, he picked it up and di-aled Amy's voice mail. It was the routine way he doled out instructions. He'd leave his assistant voice messages when-ever something came to mind, and she'd expertly handle whatever pressing matter had prompted his call. This time he wanted her to plan a wedding. How hard could it be?

Five minutes passed before his cell started in again. He answered as Amy entered his office without knocking and stood with her hands on her hips glaring at him. He stared at his petite assistant while he spoke into his phone.

"Nikki, I have work to do. Stop calling." He disconnected the call and smiled at Amy. "Nice touch with the ring-tone, but I'm done with her now. Block her number from my cell and the office phones." He raised an eyebrow, taking notice of her agitation. Her normally flawless hair style was already falling out, and the chopstick was hanging sideways. It was only eight in the morning. "Your hair is doing a thing."

She glared at him. "Really? You want to talk about my hair?"

"We could discuss when you decided it was okay to walk into my office without first knocking, if you'd rather?"

Ignoring his question, she placed both hands on his desk and leaned toward him. "You want me to plan a wedding in less than two weeks! Have you lost your mind?"

"I have confidence in you. Hire extra help if you need it."

"It'll take me two weeks just to hire the help."

"You'll think of something." He grinned. "You're the best."

"Flattery will get you nowhere this time, buster."

"Please." He changed tacks. "I'm marrying my best friend."

The short brunette let out a deep sigh. "How come I've never met this friend? What happened with you and the last one, anyway?"

7

"You never liked her, so what's it matter?"

"She wasn't right for you, but I don't see why you should rush into marriage with the next girl who comes along."

"Ames, Addison and I planned this marriage twelve years ago."

"Then why were you engaged to Nutty Nikki? Never mind. It's none of my business. I'll get started planning your wedding, but don't ask for anything else for the next two weeks."

"I'll be on my best behavior." He grinned.

"Sure you will."

"My mom will fly to the island a week early to help you with the planning." He was certain Lucinda Williams would get in Amy's way, rather than provide any meaningful assistance, but she was his mother and deserved to take part in planning his wedding.

Amy closed the door behind her with a little too much force.

Two weeks later

Running late for work, Addison slipped on her high heels and stumbled out her front door. She came face to face with Zachary Williams, hand up about to knock on the door. "Zach?" Her eyes widened in shock.

"Addison."

"Wow." She recovered and straightened her spine. "You look good."

"As do you." His azure eyes twinkled. "As always."

"Thanks." She lowered her gaze to the ground.

"Are you ready?" He held out his hand, and she placed hers inside it.

"Ready for what?" Her gaze took in the white limousine sitting in her driveway.

"Our wedding? Tomorrow morning. Did you forget I said I'd pick you up today?" They walked down the steps together.

"No. I didn't forget." Heat crept to her cheeks. "But how did you get my new address? You didn't ask for it." Maybe he hadn't been joking after all. This couldn't be happening. She should tell him she'd thought he was kidding and send him on his way. Then again, what if he'd spent a fortune on a wedding at her direction? Her conscience couldn't handle it. She got a sick feeling in the pit of her stomach. She needed to put a stop to this, she couldn't get married on a whim for no greater reason than because she'd agreed to it as a kid. It was absurd.

"I cheated. Got your address off the Fractal network."

"Well then, I'm ready, but I need to stop and pick up my dress. Can we swing by my mother's shop?"

"Isn't she coming?"

"Silly me. Yes, my mother is coming, and she'll bring my dress with her. Forgive my scattered brain." She pulled away from him and ran back up the steps to the door. "I need to call her. I'll be right back."

"Can't you call from your cell?"

"Don't you remember the spotty cell service? Give me one minute." She held up her index finger. "I'll be back in a minute."

Once inside, she leaned against the front door and tried to breathe normally. This wasn't real. It couldn't be happening. Slowly, she made her way to the cordless telephone and dialed her mother. She bounced from one foot to the other while she waited the three rings for her mother to pick up the phone. "Mom. Thank goodness you answered. The whole marriage thing wasn't a joke. Zach wasn't kidding. He's here now. I will need a wedding gown pronto, something pretty that fits me. I don't even know where to tell you to meet me. Hang on a sec."

She opened the front door. Zach stood on the top step waiting. His large frame filled her doorway, she looked up and met his eyes. "Where should I tell my mother to meet us?"

"The Wilkes-Barre/Scranton International Airport. I've arranged for my pilot to fly all of us to my private island for the ceremony."

"Okay. I'll let her know." Instead of inviting him in like a sane person, she shut the door on him and ran up the stairs with the phone still held to her ear. If she was going to go through with this insanity, she needed to pack a bag. "Mom. Meet us at the airport in Avoca and bring your passport. We're flying to a private island somewhere for the ceremony."

Five minutes later, she slid into the limo and faced Zach.

He took her hand in his. "I can see you're as nervous as I am."

"You could say that." She tried to smile but was afraid it was more of a grimace. "I haven't seen you since my father's funeral and now I'm marrying you."

"What's it been, two years?"

"Four."

"Wow. Time moves quickly. How's your mother been?" His eyebrows furrowed slightly.

"Throwing herself into her work but surviving."

"I'm glad. I've always liked your mother. She's such a sweet soul."

"You like her because she's loony."

He chuckled. "Maybe."

He squeezed her hand. "Are we crazy to be doing this?"

"Yes." She blinked rapidly as she fought the urge to jump out of the speeding car.

"Great. I need to be a little nutty to keep up the image, right?"

She giggled. "You always knew how to lighten the mood." Her eyes met his. "Are we seriously doing this?"

"If you're willing?" He pulled a velvet box out of his pocket and held it out to her.

She admired the emerald-cut diamond briefly before meeting his eyes. Her voice came out in a whisper. "I'm willing."

He removed the ring from the box and placed it on the ring finger of her left hand. The enormity of what she'd agreed to hit her. He was Zachary. Her closest friend in the world, but after all this time, he was a stranger. If she followed through with this, she would live her life in the limelight, the wife of a billionaire entrepreneur.

It would mean quitting her job and living in Beverly Hills. If she didn't work, how would she fill her days? The questions bombarded her one after another making normal breathing impossible. Oh, no. Work. She hadn't called them.

"Hey." He stroked her hair and stared into her eyes. "Don't panic. We're in this together. As always."

"Together." She smiled. "More now than ever before, huh?"

He laughed. "I would say so."

Traffic was light on the ride to the airport. After a few minutes of chatter, Addison grew quiet. Zach stole a sideways glance at her. In the black pencil skirt and pink blouse, she was slightly overdressed, but so was he since he'd had an early morning meeting with his second-in-command before leaving for the airport. He had to make sure everything was properly handled while he was away.

Addison was prettier than he remembered. She must've straightened her hair as it didn't have a hint of the wave he recalled. Her dark eyes seemed disquieted, but when he tried to make eye contact, she quickly turned away.

Maybe he should worry about her pensiveness, but his gut told him this was the right decision for both of them. Once they spent a little time together, her trepidation would decrease. It might help if he could get her to talk about it, then maybe he could ease whatever fears she was having.

"You still do that?" She looked at his hand pointedly.

"What?"

"Drum on things when you're nervous."

"I guess it's my tell." He stopped drumming.

"I remember the many evenings I sat alone outside of your drum teacher's house while you practiced."

"I wasn't terrible."

"You were good." She smiled. "Too bad you didn't do anything with it."

"I was in the marching band."

She let out a choked laugh. "True. It was quite the band. What did we have, ten kids most of whom played their instruments off-key?"

"Eight and we were dreadful. I think it was more about timing than key though." He bounced his leg slightly. "Are you ready for this?"

"Not really. I'm glad to see you're nervous. I'm a wreck."

"What's causing your anxiety?"

"Running off to a private island somewhere to marry a man I haven't even dated." She held her purse in a death grip.

He pried her fingers off her handbag and laced his fingers through hers. "It's not like you don't know me."

"Do I though? I'm sure you've changed."

"I don't think so. Have you?"

"Yes. I know I have."

He released her hand when the car came to a stop. The driver got out to open his door, but he beat him to it and hurried around the car to assist Addison. She slipped out before he reached her side of the car.

Honestly, he was having his own doubts, but there was no way he'd give up the chance to marry the only honest woman he knew. It wasn't possible for them to date like normal people when they lived on opposite sides of the country. He was certain that if he offered to move her to California, so he could court her, she'd balk at the idea. Addison Scott wouldn't be willing to uproot her life for anything less than marriage. So, that's what he was offering.

Chapter 2

Carolyn Scott arrived at the airport in her signature flamboyant manner dressed in a flowing zebra-striped dress with chunky bright-red jewelry. It wasn't something Addison would choose for an airplane ride. Unlike her mother, she preferred comfort to fashion. Addison did a double take when she noticed Parker in a conservative gray suit, her long blond hair pulled tightly into a bun. She hadn't been expecting her sister.

When they reached Addison, a cloud of Tiffany perfume prompted a sneezing fit. Her mother grabbed her by the wrist and dragged her into the ladies' room, and her sister trailed behind. "We'll need to make adjustments tonight, so your dress will fit properly in the morning."

Her mother caught sight of the ring and snatched up her hand. "Let me see that thing!" She stared at the enormous diamond and then waved Parker over to look at it. "It's gorgeous."

"You don't think it's too big for my hand?"

"That's not a complaint most women would have. You'll get used to it." Parker waved her off and walked to the mirror to touch up her lipstick.

Addison dabbed her nose with a tissue she'd scrounged up in her purse. "May I see the dress?" She hoped it would suit her and not be something in her mother's style.

"I think you'll like it." She pulled it from the garment bag. "It's definitely not something I would wear, but it's understated and elegant, so I thought it would suit your style."

One look at the dress, and she sent up a prayer of gratitude. It was a lovely white sheath dress with white lace overlaying it. "It's gorgeous, mother." She placed a hand on her mother's arm. "Absolutely perfect. I couldn't have chosen better myself. There's a reason your fashion advice is in high demand." Her mother's clothing store overflowed with women seeking her guidance, even though her own fashion was often over-the-top, she could spend five minutes with someone and know what suited them best. It was a gift. She wondered why she'd doubted her, even for a second. Parker stood quietly to the side inspecting her nails.

Addison fished her cell phone out of her purse and sent a text to her boss. "My boss is going to hate me. At least I finished the Garrison Security website. Mom, tell me I'm making a mistake." She bit her bottom lip nervously. "Tell me to call it off."

"You'd be a fool to cancel this wedding."

"How can you say that? Don't you think I should marry for love?"

Parker laughed. "Love? You are naïve. Love doesn't last."

Addison didn't respond, her sister and Ben married young, and it turned out poorly when he ran off and left her with a mountain of debt. They'd been separated for two years, so her bitterness was only natural.

She was grateful when her mother broke the uncomfortable silence. "Zach has been your best friend since you were in diapers. Do you think it's possible to love another human being more than you do him?"

"It's not like that with Zach and me. We've never shared any kind of romantic feelings, certainly not love." She continued gnawing on her lip. "There's no passion between us." At least not for him. Her thoughts strayed back to high school and the nights she'd lain awake dreaming of him. He hadn't returned her feelings then, and she'd do well to remember that he felt nothing for her now. To him this was a mutually beneficial arrangement. It was not a love match. If she was to survive the experience without severe emotional scars, she would need to keep her heart out of it. She could stay cool and detached if she set her mind to it. Even as she thought the words, she knew she was deluding herself. It would be impossible to stay detached to a man she'd married. Especially a man like Zachary Williams, one glance at his dimples and she'd be a goner. It would be high school all over again.

"There can be passion if you let it develop." Her mother pulled her in for another hug. "I think you two will bring each other happiness."

"Maybe I should insist on a longer engagement."

"Nonsense. Everything is set. All you have to do is get on that private jet and show up at your wedding. You cannot imagine how much stress he's saved you by having this wedding planned out for you."

"I'm sorry I didn't warn you about this. I honestly believed this was a joke."

"I didn't." Her mother smiled warmly. "Your dress didn't come from the stock I had on hand. I special ordered it the day you told me about Zachary's 'joke.' Even in jest, you wouldn't have said yes if you didn't want this at least subconsciously."

"You might be right." She lifted a hand to her hair and noticed the shaking. "I'm frightened."

"I should hope so."

"You confuse me, Mom. If you think I should go through with this, why would you hope for me to be scared?"

"It means you're taking this marriage business seriously."

Zach waited for Addison beside the steps leading up to his private jet. She'd been whispering with her mother and sister since they'd emerged from the restroom. They were in there for what felt like an eternity, and he wondered what they'd been doing. He was apprehensive, so surely, she was harboring doubts. Hopefully, her family wasn't trying to talk her out of marrying him. Starting the search for a wife again wasn't something he was prepared to do. This had to succeed.

When she reached the stairs, he took her hand and leaned down to whisper in her ear. "If you're having second thoughts, I'll understand." It wasn't true, but it was the polite thing to say. This was something he wanted badly, even knowing it was a crazy idea. She stood beside him as her family boarded the airplane.

When she shook her head, the tension that had been keeping his body rigid released a tad, and he took a deep breath. He waited for her to climb the steps and followed behind her. He escorted her to a seat and waited for her to sit before settling in beside her.

"Tan leather couches on a plane?"

He settled in beside her. "They have seat belts. Don't look so worried."

"Aren't you scared?" She squeezed his hand.

"Only that you'll change your mind."

"My mother reminded me that you're my best friend, and that there was no better foundation than friendship on which to start a marriage."

"She's a wise woman." He glanced over at her mother and grinned. "Thanks, Mrs. Scott."

"Anytime, sweetie pie."

"Have I told you lately how much I like your mom?"

She gave him a crooked grin and laughed. "How could you? We haven't so much as spoken on the telephone in years."

"True." He returned her smile. "I can't imagine why we lost touch."

"We have separate lives on opposite coasts."

"I guess we must mesh them now, huh?"

She spoke quietly to keep her family from overhearing her. "I'm not naïve, Zach. I'm aware that it will be my life that has to change."

"I appreciate your directness."

"Let's hope you find other stuff about me to appreciate."

"Like your mother said, you're my best friend."

"No. I believe she said *you* were *my* best friend. I'm sure you've made many more friends over the years."

"Not true. I have an assistant who is a friend, sort of. I confide in her, but she can't be a true friend. Not like you.

19

She's a paid employee, so she'll never be truly free to speak her mind knowing I have the power to fire her."

"I suppose that's true." She stared up at him. "You don't have any other close friends?"

"No. I don't."

"Me neither."

"We have each other." He reached for her hand and laced his fingers through hers.

They passed the time on the flight catching up. When they arrived on the island, Zach led them up to the house.

"As you can see, I had the house built with reinforced concrete to withstand the violent storms common to the area."

"It's beautiful. Gives the place the feel of a fairytale castle." Addison looked out over the white sand to the waves lapping the shore. "It's a far cry from Fenwick."

"I hope you like it."

"I do."

He ascended the stairs and opened the front door for them. "It's so open."

"Yes. I had it designed that way, so I could talk to my guests from the kitchen."

"Don't you have staff who do most of your cooking?"

"I do, but I enjoy cooking, so I spend a good deal of time in there myself."

"Do you have many guests on your island?" Parker asked.

He chuckled. "Only occasionally. I have flown people out here for business functions. There have been a few times when I've invited other visitors."

Her attempt to fish for information was humorous, but he would not come right out and mention that Addison wasn't the first woman he'd brought to the island. Some things were best left unsaid.

It was nice seeing the place fresh through their eyes as they commented on the decor throughout the tour. He stopped at one of the guest rooms. "This will be your room, Mrs. Scott."

Carolyn Scott wandered to the window and looked out over the rocks below. "It's a lovely view."

"Addison will be in the adjoining room, and Parker you'll be across the hall from your mother, next door to my mom."

He held open a door that connected the two rooms. "My mother flew out a week early." They followed him from the room, and he led them down the hall to the master suite in the west wing of the house.

Addison gaped at the king-sized bed, and her face turned a lovely shade of pink. It was adorable. He hadn't come across many women who could be made to blush so easily.

He showed them the den and the game room and then opened the sliding glass doors to the beach, Parker didn't join them, claiming she felt a migraine coming on. A few minutes later, Mrs. Scott looked back at the house. "I'm going to go check on Parker. I'll see you two a little later." He recognized her attempt to allow them alone time and appreciated the gesture.

He took Addison's hand in his and led her down to the water's edge. As they walked together, he prayed. Her reluctance was clear, so he wasn't sure why she'd agreed to marry him. She wasn't money hungry, so it couldn't be that, but he wanted more from her than tentative acceptance. He wanted to persuade her to open her heart to possibilities. It was his intention to ferret out her motives and determine if they had a chance for a real marriage. One afternoon alone in the rain forest may not be enough to be certain of her feelings, but it would help them reconnect and give her a chance to pull out of their deal if she were so inclined.

"Do you trust me?" he asked.

She searched his eyes. "Yes."

"Then come with me."

"Come with you where?" She smiled hesitantly. "I flew across the ocean to your private island. How much farther do you want me to go?"

"We need time alone."

"Where?"

"Not far, but we'll be alone with no staff and no future in-laws."

"Works for me."

"I'll have you home by midnight."

"Sounds a tad late for our wedding night. My mom wants to do a final fitting for my dress."

"Let's go back up to the house. She can do the fitting now, and then we'll go." He grinned. "I'll have you all to myself."

She let out a choked laugh. "Isn't that what honeymoons are for?"

He chuckled at her directness. "Definitely, but that wasn't the type of quality time to which I was referring. I was thinking more along the lines of time for us to get reacquainted."

Chapter 3

Addison's nervousness grew as she climbed onto the ATV behind Zach and held onto his waist. She could feel her face warm with embarrassment again as she felt his muscles tighten at her touch. It was bizarre being so close to him after so many years apart. Even so, it felt strangely fitting.

"Where are we going?" She raised her voice to be heard over the roar of the engine.

"Don't worry the island isn't large, I won't get you lost."

"I wasn't worried." A smile formed when he took off, and the wind whipped her hair around her face. She let herself enjoy the moment.

A steady mist covered them, as he drove into the rain forest before veering off the trail and following a barely visible rocky path. He came to a stop at the bottom of an enormous tree. "You ready?"

"Ready for what?" It was then that she noticed the rope ladder. "I'm not going up that thing."

"It's a tree house." He grinned. "You'll love it. It'll be like we're kids again."

"I feel like a kid when I'm with you."

"Trust me." He climbed a few steps up and jumped back down. "You go first. I'll climb up after you, so I can catch you if you fall."

"You're not making your case by reminding me that I might fall."

"Chicken."

The taunt worked. "Fine." She grabbed onto the rope and climbed, one step at a time, not looking down. She knew he was standing below watching to be sure she was safe, but her stomach twisted in knots.

When she reached the top, she pulled herself up and looked around. The views of the island from the top were breathtaking.

He joined her less than a minute later. "What do you think?"

"The views are spectacular." She turned to admire the house. "I can't believe you have an entire house in the tops of the trees." She shook her head while she looked around his open-air home. "This is ludicrous. Your tree house is better equipped than my everyday house."

He grinned. "Do you like it?"

"Yes, but why have it? What's wrong with your other house?"

"Nothing. The main house is great, but this is my private space. I come here when I want to be alone. Nobody else is permitted in here."

"Then, I suppose you clean it yourself?"

He chuckled. "Great point. I have a housekeeper who keeps it dusted and vacuumed when I'm away, so she *is* allowed inside, but she doesn't come here when I'm on the island. Her husband is my maintenance guy."

"If it's your private spot, why did you bring me here?"

"You're the first person I've wanted to share it with." He stared into her eyes.

"That's sweet." She broke eye contact and walked out on the deck. "I feel special."

He followed her. "How many times have I told you that you're special?"

"You were only being kind."

"Was I only being kind the night I kissed you after prom?"

"It was a pity kiss. You felt sorry for me when my date left with another girl."

"Is that why you avoided me after that? You thought I pitied you?"

"I don't know what you mean. I didn't avoid you."

"Yes, you did." He turned her around to face him. "Did you honestly think I would kiss you out of pity?"

Her eyes welled up. "I did."

He took both her hands in his and she tried to ignore the jolt of excitement his touch provoked. "Why would you think such a thing?"

She pulled her hands away. "Why wouldn't I think it? That entire year I practically threw myself at you. I gave you every indication that I was interested in being more than friends, but you ignored my advances until that night."

"That's not fair." He stood and stalked over to the railing. "One of us was always in another relationship. Whenever I was single, you were dating someone. The night I kissed you, I was with Carly. I'd already taken her home from prom when you called me crying. The next morning I went to her house and ended it with her so you and I could date, but you avoided me from that day forward. That kiss was a death knell for our friendship."

"I didn't want to give you a chance to tell me that your kiss meant nothing."

"It meant everything to me, but I believed you avoided me because the head cheerleader couldn't be seen with a chess club geek. I guess we both had our insecurities, but its ancient history now."

"Yep." Her stomach plummeted to the floor. She could've been dating Zach the entire last month of high school had she not been so fearful. Who knows where it might've led? "What are we doing here, Zach?"

"Following through on our pledge to each other." He sauntered back over to her and looked into her eyes. "It's not too late to back out, Addison. If you don't want to be here, say the word and you'll be forever free of me."

"I don't want to be free of you." She swallowed hard and forced herself not to turn away from the intensity in his eyes. "I will not back out." As crazy as this plan was, it would be crazier to ruin another chance at happiness with him.

"Are you sure you want this?"

How could she be sure? They hadn't seen each other in years, and she was planning to say 'I do' the following morning. She chose not to answer. Instead, she turned her gaze away from him. Maybe marrying him would turn out fine. She hoped so. Otherwise, she was making a huge mistake that could ruin both of their futures.

Addison sat on a stool and watched as Zach prepared a picnic dinner. He sliced cheese, cut up fruit, and added bread to the pack.

"I can't believe you have a full kitchen in your tree house." She twirled a piece of hair around her index finger. "Where are we going for our picnic?"

He stopped what he was doing and watched her a moment before answering. "There's a waterfall close to here. I thought you might enjoy seeing it."

"I didn't bring a raincoat."

He laughed. "You won't need one. It doesn't always rain in the rain forest, but if the rain picks up, as warm as it is, it'll feel good, and I promise you won't melt."

She rolled her eyes. He descended the rope ladder first, and waited, so he could catch her if she slipped. After she jumped the last two feet and was firmly planted on the ground, she peered up at him. "Why not get something more stable, maybe a wooden or aluminum ladder?"

"It's a thought, but I kind of like things the way they are."

"Humph."

She could tell he was holding in a chuckle. Probably didn't want to annoy the woman he was marrying in the morning.

The sun was setting when they arrived at the waterfall. Her eyes widened and she stared at the magnificent rushing water. "Wow."

"My sentiments exactly."

"I've seen nothing like it."

"You've been to Niagara Falls."

"It's not the same, that whole area is built up and touristy, this is pure, unadulterated."

He rested his hand on her shoulder and stared at the rushing water. "I'm fond of it."

"Don't you feel bad about having it all to yourself?"

"Sometimes, I do. Then I think about what they've done to other natural wonders and I'm glad it's protected. I hope to find a way to share it, but in the meantime, the beauty will be preserved for future generations."

"I guess that makes sense."

"There's a flat rock over there. Follow me, and we'll set up dinner." He led the way and spread out the blanket he'd brought.

She stared at the blanket. "Won't that get soaked?"

"With this material it won't matter."

She leaned down to touch the material and was surprised at its texture.

"The water will bead up and roll off."

"If you say so." She lowered herself onto the rock and helped him unpack their light dinner. "I'm glad you didn't want a heavy meal. I'm too nervous to eat much."

"There's nothing to be nervous about. I'll treat you well. I promise."

"I know that. I just hope you know what you're doing."

"I do."

She silently thanked God for the meal. A gentle mist sprayed her face while she picked at her food. The view was amazing, but as beautiful as the waterfall was, she found herself drawn to the sounds of the rain forest: tropical birds screeching overhead and water crashing loudly against the rocks. It was peaceful in Zach's paradise. Any woman would be blessed to spend time with such a handsome man in this wild and beautiful place, but she couldn't understand why he'd picked her. The man could have almost any woman he wanted. Why choose her? There wasn't anything special about Addison Scott.

Zach's stomach tightened into a hard knot as he watched Addison pick at her food.

How could he be sure she wanted to be here with him when she was so unreadable? He was certain his plan would work out perfectly one instant, but the next minute he thought she'd run away if he so much as turned his head. If she had misgivings, he wanted to hear them, and he'd told her as much, but she wasn't sharing her feelings.

"You don't seem interested in your food. Want to pack up and go have some fun?"

"It's getting dark out here."

"I'll keep my promise to have you home by midnight."

"You're making me feel like Cinderella."

"I wouldn't ask you to cook and clean."

"I don't mind household chores, Zach."

"I didn't say you couldn't cook and clean if you wanted to, I said I wouldn't ask you to. Besides, you fit more into the role of Belle in Beauty and the Beast."

"Does that make you a beast?" She laughed.

"Maybe, but I was thinking more of her affinity for books and libraries. Wait until you see the library at my place, you'll be in heaven."

He cherished the dreamy look in her eyes, but it soon faded away, and apprehension once again took its place. "I'm surprised you remember that movie."

"Your sister watched it every day for a year. How could I forget it?"

"True enough. It's burned into my brain."

"So which are you? Cinderella or Belle?" He leaned away from her, so he could study her as she answered.

"Belle, I think. I enjoy thinking of you as my beast, but tonight I guess I'm Cinderella with the whole midnight thing."

He scooted closer to her and held her gaze. "I'm not a beast, Addison, but if that's how you see me, I'm glad you're my Belle."

She didn't respond. "What if you were to lose everything? Then, I'll bet you'd expect me to cook and clean like Cinderella."

"If I were to lose everything, I'd be the same Zach you've always known, and I'm capable of cooking and cleaning, although I'd be grateful for your help."

"Then it's a good thing I don't mind housework."

He studied her for a moment. "Would you leave me if I lost everything?"

"What a dumb thing to ask. You know me better than that. How can you even insinuate that I'd marry you for the money?" Her expressive brown eyes bored into his with an intensity he didn't quite fathom. He sensed she needed something from him, but he couldn't discern what that might be.

She stood on the deck of the tree house and stared at the barely visible zip line, shaking her head. "No way am I zip lining in the dark."

"It might be fun, but it wasn't what I had in mind for tonight. Let's do that tomorrow."

"You want me to go zip lining on our wedding day?"

"Definitely."

She grimaced. "If that's what you want to do, I'll try it."

"I like that about you."

"What?"

"That you're willing to try new things even when you're scared."

"Who says I'm scared?"

"I can see the fear in your eyes." He disappeared for a few minutes, and she took the opportunity to enjoy the dense jungle surrounding her. It smelled like wet earth and flowers. Taking a deep breath of the moist air, she listened to the chorus of frogs and insects. Everything about the rain forest at night seemed magical.

Soon music came through unseen speakers. When he returned, he held his arms out to her. "Will you dance with me, Addison Scott?"

She stepped into his embrace. "I won't be Addison Scott much longer, will I?"

"No. Tomorrow morning you'll be Mrs. Zachary Williams."

"It sounds posh and snobbish."

He chuckled, and she could feel the vibrations from his laugh. Being close to Zach felt nice, but it seemed too good to be true. If he wanted to marry her, he had to have a hidden agenda even if she couldn't figure out what that might be. Marrying her billionaire buddy wouldn't be a hardship by any means, but what if his motives weren't pure? Not that she could imagine anything he might want from her since she had nothing to offer. So, she hoped against hope that everything was as it seemed.

She let herself relax into the dance and moved to the music following his lead.

One dance turned into another, and he leaned down to whisper in her ear. "I'm glad we're doing this."

"Dancing?" She gazed up into his sparkling blue eyes.

"Getting married."

She gave a slight shrug. "I wish I had your confidence."

"There is nobody in the world I would rather take this leap with."

"I find that hard to believe, Zach."

"What made you so cynical, Addison?"

She ignored his question but edged closer to him. If he was going to dance with her, she intended to enjoy every second of the experience. The rain picked up, but he made no move to go inside. When the next song started, she stared into his eyes. "Shouldn't we get out of the weather?"

"No. We shouldn't." He grinned but didn't break eye contact. "We have little time left, Cinderella. Let's make tonight memorable. How many times have you danced in the rain?"

"This is my first."

His eyes traveled to her lips, and she looked away feeling suddenly uncomfortable. It was more than she'd expected. He was treating this like a real romance. It would be wise to back out now, but she couldn't bring herself to walk away from him.

Zach didn't want the night to end. Holding Addison in his arms on the deck of his tree house in paradise felt wonderful, and he wanted the moment to last forever. The way she fit in his arms, made him feel like she was designed just for him. He twirled her around and she smiled, but her smile didn't reach her eyes.

Something in her eyes remained guarded despite his efforts to reassure her they would be great together. He didn't doubt that she'd stand beside him tomorrow morning and say 'I do,' but he was wondering if she wanted to be his wife or if some sense of duty was behind the choice. Maybe for her this was about getting older and worrying that she wouldn't find her Mr. Right in time to start a family. That he could definitely understand. It was part of what prompted him to contact her.

He dipped her, and she giggled. Seeing her smile made everything feel right. It might take time, but he intended to prove to her that he was the man she needed, and that she could count on him.

The rain soaked them, but he kept dancing brushing off her initial protests. Before long, she relaxed and seemed to enjoy herself.

"It's time to head back, Cinderella."

"Is it getting late, already?"

"It is, and I promised you I'd have you home by midnight."

"Maybe we should find out if I will turn into a pumpkin."

"It was the carriage that changed, princess."

"That's true."

"I'm confident the quad won't turn into a pumpkin, but I should still get you back." He kept dancing and didn't release her.

"That will be difficult to do while dancing." She pulled out of his arms, but her smile seemed genuine.

"I'm not ready for the night to end."

"Me neither."

He headed down the rope ladder first and waited at the bottom for her to join him. Taking her hand in his, he led her to the quad which blended into the dark jungle. "Hang on tight. I don't want to lose you in the dark."

"Don't worry. I will."

His muscles contracted as her delicate fingers grasped his waist. If they weren't getting married, she would be his undoing for sure. He smiled as he felt the ring on her left hand. It was a short engagement, but she was his fiancée. Tomorrow morning, Addison Scott would finally belong to him. It had been a long time since his first crush on her in fifth grade, but she continued to hold his interest, and soon she'd be his.

Chapter 4

Soaking wet and laughing, they jumped off the ATV and ran toward the house. Addison shivered when they walked into the air-conditioned living space.

"We made it in the nick of time, Cinderella." Zach grinned.

"Less than a minute to spare." She shivered again, and he tugged on her hand. "Come on. Let's get you dry."

"I should probably go to my room and change." She started down the hall but turned back to face him. "I'll be back."

Five minutes later, she joined him in the living room after changing into capris and a t-shirt.

He patted the couch, and she settled in beside him, curling her feet under her. "Did you have a nice time today?"

"I did. It was nice catching up."

"That's something you say to someone you don't plan on seeing again. Is there something I should know? Are you having second thoughts?"

"I'm having third thoughts and fourth thoughts, but I'm not leaving unless you want me to go."

"That's a relief."

"You keep asking me if I trust you, but it's clear you don't trust me."

"I have serious trust issues."

"Clearly. I think it's the tenth time you've asked me if I want to back out."

"You're exaggerating." He grinned.

"Only slightly."

"Do you want to watch television?"

"Not really. We should probably get some sleep."

"We should, but I'm too wound up to sleep."

"Me too." She rested her head against the sofa. "I'm crazy nervous. I always thought I'd marry for love after a long courtship and engagement."

"Same here."

"So, why *are* we doing this?"

"Time is short. I've wasted more than enough of it with the dating scene. I want a family, Addison. I know you do too."

She swallowed. His reasons were sound. It was fine to marry for practicality's sake. It didn't have to be a love match. Love could grow, couldn't it? They weren't short on physical attraction. At least not on her end. Just being near him caused the butterflies in her stomach to do a polka. She wasn't sure if he found her attractive or not. Maybe that kiss in high school wasn't a pity kiss, but it had been a long time since high school, and she was no longer a perky cheerleader.

He grinned like he'd read her mind. "Milk and cookies?"

"I thought you'd never ask."

They entered the kitchen, and Zach got out the Oreos and set them out on the breakfast bar. He poured them each a glass of milk before pulling a stool out for her. She hopped up on it and dunked her first cookie. For the next ten minutes, they sat side by side eating their cookies and milk. If she didn't want to exacerbate her blood sugar problems, she'd have to be sure they didn't make the childhood ritual a regular habit, but it was fun to revert to old times for a moment.

Zach wiped his mouth with a napkin. "I don't know if you heard the weather reports, but we should be safe here if the hurricane stays on its current track."

"Back up. A hurricane? How would I hear anything, I've been with you all day?" She shook her head. "When did you find out about this?"

"Shortly after we landed, while you were in your room changing."

She folded her arms over her chest. "Why didn't you tell me?"

"Don't stress over it. Stay calm."

She shook her head. "Don't tell me to be calm when there's a hurricane coming."

"It's not supposed to hit for another two days and it should miss us entirely."

"Humph." She pushed her chair out and stood.

He blew out a breath. "We have plenty of time to decide what to do."

"I can't believe you didn't tell me." She paced back and forth.

"I'm sorry." He frowned. "I should've told you immediately."

She stopped in her tracks and turned to face him. "Are we in danger?"

"I don't think so." He drummed his fingers on the table. "We can decide how to proceed in the morning. If after the wedding, the reports suggest it might veer our way, and we think it's not safe to stay here, we can leave the island with the guests and staff."

She forced a smile. "I'm going to bed." Turning on her heel, she headed for her room.

Zach stared at Addison's retreating back. He'd blown it this time. He should've mentioned the approaching storm, but his first instinct was to keep it from her. He'd thought of how his ex would react and waited to tell her. It wasn't fair of him to compare her to Nikki when the two were nothing alike.

His mother came in the back door, and he glanced her way. "I didn't know you were outside, Mom."

"I sat on the patio and waited for you to return. I didn't want to interrupt the two of you, but I was hoping to see you before you went to bed. Addison seemed upset, is everything all right?"

"There is a storm coming, and I hadn't told her about it, so she was a little ticked at me." He sat down at the table. "Is something wrong, Mom?"

"Not at all. I only wanted to talk to my only son before he got married." She sat beside him.

"Do you think I'm making a mistake?" His fingers drummed out a beat on the table.

She put her hand on top of his to still him. "I honestly don't know. What I know is that you've loved that girl since before you were old enough to know what love meant."

"Don't make this something it's not, mother. It's simple. I'm sick of playing games, and Addison feels the same way. Love has nothing to do with this marriage. It's about finding someone I can trust to build a life with. None of the women I've dated are as candid and without guile as Addison."

"As long as you're both sure that's what you want, then I'm happy for you."

"She's not as convinced as I am." He tugged at the hem of his shirt.

"I wouldn't be so sure about that. She's here isn't she?"

"Reluctantly, but yes."

"You could postpone the wedding."

"I could."

"But you're not going to?"

"No."

"In that case, I hope your marriage is a blessed union."

"Mom, why didn't you ever date again after Dad left?"

"Because we remain married."

"You could've asked for a divorce."

"Divorce is not in my DNA. Are you worried that you'll make the same mistakes your father did?"

"Maybe a little. I love my Dad, but I don't understand how he could leave. I get that he was unhappy. I mean, life can be hard, and I'm sure it's easier to run away sometimes, but I still don't get him."

"You don't have to. You're not him, and you know the devastation his mistakes caused, so I doubt you'd make the same decisions he did."

"Thanks. I needed to hear that."

"Why isn't he here, Zachary?"

"I invited him, but with the short notice he didn't think he'd be able to get the time off work, and I have a feeling Debbie convinced him not to try."

"Well, I wish he was here for you. You deserve to have both parents present at your wedding."

"It's fine. I'm glad you're here, and Mrs. Scott and Parker are like family too, so I've got all the family I need."

"Addison is a lucky girl. You're a fine young man, Zachary."

"I love you, Mom."

"I love you. Now get some sleep, so you'll be ready for your big day tomorrow."

"I'll try, but I doubt I'll be able to sleep."

"Like a little boy on Christmas Eve?"

"Very much like that."

"Goodnight, Zachary." His mother hugged him and gave him a kiss on the cheek before heading off to bed.

He resumed his drumming on the table and thought about the day to come.

Addison awakened with a sick feeling in the pit of her stomach. She wondered if she was making a huge mistake. Could the friendship she had with Zach become the romance she'd dreamed about?

His clear penetrating eyes came to mind, and she flopped back on the bed. How many nights in high school had she dreamed about him holding her? Despite his claims, she knew that she'd only ever been a friend to him. All the evenings spent on the beach listening to him talk about his latest flame left no room for doubt. Anytime her traitorous heart thought there was a chance, she'd quashed the notion immediately, knowing that his heart was not inclined toward her. What had changed? Why was he suddenly willing to settle for her?

The man differed from the boy she'd known. His decisiveness was exciting, but also terrifying. She was putting everything on the line and taking a risk that he wouldn't change his mind. As a Christian, her heart was God's first, and if she committed to a marriage with Zach, she wouldn't be the one to break that promise. If they married each other today, they were in it for life unless he backed out. Maybe life on the West Coast had hardened him, and he'd be less determined to keep his vows.

She stood and crossed the room to the closet. Her wedding gown hung there in a clear garment bag. After unzipping the bag, she removed the dress and held it in front of her before the floor-length mirror. A knock came from the adjoining room. "Come in, Mom."

"Darling, you can't put your dress on yet. You must eat something first."

"I don't think I can eat." She laid a hand on her stomach to still the butterflies.

"I'll bring up a tray with a light breakfast. The groom can't see the bride before the wedding, so you can't go downstairs."

"I said I can't eat, Mom," she snapped.

Her mother put her hands on her hips and lifted her chin. "I don't care how old you get; you will not speak to your mother that way."

"Then stop babying me."

"You'd better improve your attitude by the time I return." Her mother stalked across the room and left by the door to the hall instead of returning to her own room.

Addison sat on the edge of the bed and shook her head. What was she doing here? Her wedding day should be full of joy, but she felt trepidation as she entered a loveless marriage. Well not loveless exactly, they'd once been close friends, but that was so long ago that it felt like another lifetime. Walking to the window she called out to God for peace. The ocean seemed endless its waves lapping gently against the white sand beach. It was impossible to believe the weather reports that a hurricane was headed this way. The beauty of the day made the thought seem absurd.

Her spirits lifted at the sight of the staff setting up flowers and chairs along the beach. If she didn't want to miss her own wedding, she'd need to get ready. She quickly showered and applied her makeup. When the knock came, she poked herself in the eye with her eyeliner. Moving to the door, she opened it a crack to see who it was. Her mother pushed the door open and breezed in with four other women following her.

"Mom, I'm not dressed. Who are these people?"

"Don't be rude, Addison." Her mother smiled that plastic smile she gave customers. "My daughter isn't used to so much attention." She spoke to the other women.

Turning back to Addison, she said, "You know Zachary's mother, Lucinda Williams, though you haven't seen each other in years." Addison smiled and returned the hug Mrs. Williams gave her. "These ladies are Jenn, Jill, and Jess, whoever hired them, must've wanted to cause as much confusion as possible. They'll be doing your hair and makeup and helping you with whatever else you need."

"Sorry. Zach mentioned none of this. I did my makeup already."

Jenn took her by the chin and inspected her face. "It's not terrible. We can work with it." She walked toward the vanity. "Come sit." She pointed to a soft padded chair.

Following behind them was Jess. "Do you want to wear your hair up or down? Curls or no curls?"

"Up, I think," she answered. After five minutes more of them peppering her with questions, she let herself relax and enjoy the pampering.

When an hour had passed, and her hair and makeup were flawless. Jill pulled out a jewelry case and held earrings up to see which she liked. Jill convinced her to wear dangling rubies surrounded by tiny diamond chips. They were way out of her comfort zone. Her mother loved them. Enough said. But, if she could fly to a private island in the Bahamas and marry a man she hadn't seen in years, leaving her simple life in Pennsylvania's farm country behind, she could wear a pair of extravagant earrings too. Addison Scott was reinventing herself. She was a new woman.

When the time came to dress, everyone seemed eager to offer assistance. She squeezed herself into the shapewear her mother insisted she needed. Then came another layer that flared out slightly at the bottom. She supposed it was a slip or a crinoline of some sort but wasn't sure what to call it.

When it came time to put on her actual wedding gown, she felt her throat close with panic, but her mother put her hands on her shoulders, calming her. "You look lovely, my dear. Come. See." She pulled her over to the full-length mirror. Seeing her full transformation for the first time was a shock. She felt as beautiful as a fairy-tale princess.

Chapter 5

It was time. Zach breathed in a deep breath of the fresh sea air and watched a gull swoop overhead as he stood on the beach beside the preacher. Soon the woman he would spend the rest of his life with would walk down the white sand beach toward him and they would start a new journey together. His nerves were on edge. He glanced out at the rows of chairs filled with family, colleagues, and staff. The whole experience seemed surreal.

This was a step he hadn't dreamed of taking with Addison, but the more extensively he dated, the more he realized that other women couldn't measure up to his childhood friend. Most of them wanted to play games and keep secrets. Yet, now that he was about to take this step, uncertainty niggled at the back of his mind. What if she had changed? He saw no evidence of change in the areas that mattered, but she claimed to be a different person.

He pushed his doubts away and watched her descend the steps from the patio, a lovely vision in white lace. The moment she reached the sand, she kicked off her heels. The gesture brought a smile to his face. It was a trivial thing, but it showed her nature. She was the same girl he remembered despite her assertions to the contrary.

She carried a bouquet of purple and yellow flowers he couldn't name. They were ideal for her. Simple, so unlike the elaborate flower arrangements she strolled past on her way to his side. Their mothers sat together, both teary eyed. Nobody walked his bride down the aisle. If she'd married another man, the responsibility might've fallen to him now that her father was gone, but it relieved him that he wouldn't be asked to give Addison Scott to another man.

She might not know it yet, but they were doing the right thing, he was nearly convinced of it. In time she would see that they were meant to be together. If he let this opportunity pass him by, he'd be a fool. When she reached him, he stretched his hands out for hers, but she seemed unsure what to do with her bouquet. Her mother stood halfway out of her seat and reached up to take it. He wondered why her sister hadn't played the part of a bridesmaid for her. Forcing himself back into the moment, he grinned at the beautiful woman by his side, but the smile she returned was tentative.

When Zach reached for her hands, Addison panicked and nearly pulled away. Her mother grabbed for her bouquet and smiled reassuringly. Taking a steadying breath she handed the flowers off and placed her hands in Zach's.

This was it. The moment of truth where childhood friends would commit their lives to each other for better or for worse. Her heart raced as she stared into his clear azure eyes.

The preacher said something, but she didn't hear over the buzzing in her head. Shaking herself mentally, she looked away from her groom and tried to focus on the pastor. Zach repeated the preacher's words, and she followed suit.

Once they'd spoken their vows, and Zach slipped the ring on her finger, the gravity of the moment hit her, and tears threatened. She placed the ring on his finger, and he bent to kiss her. His lips barely brushed against hers, but the sensations his kiss evoked left her feeling even more off-kilter.

She stood beside her husband and they waited as a line of people formed to congratulate them. The word husband rolled around in her head, foreign and strange. Ha! She was a wife. That word might be even harder to get used to. It seemed odd to her that the line was so long when she hadn't realized there were so many people on the island. Her mother and sister were the first to approach.

"I know you'll bring each other great joy. Nothing could bring a mother more pleasure than knowing her daughter will be taken care of by a good-hearted man." Her mother hugged Zach.

Parker gave her an awkward hug. "I'm glad you're happy. You deserve it." The sadness in her sister's eyes belied her words, but she accepted her remarks with grace rather than question her sincerity.

When her family moved on, she noticed an enormous ship in the distant that appeared to be drawing near the island. She turned to stare at the approaching vessel. "What's this?"

"I chartered a cruise ship for our guests and employees."

"Aren't they staying here on the island?"

"I offered them a seven-day cruise. A few are flying back to the mainland, but most are taking advantage of the free vacation."

Her hand flew to her throat. "Why didn't I know about this?"

"I thought your mother would've mentioned it. She's going."

"Are we going with them?"

He chuckled. "No, we're staying here, but it'll be just the two of us."

She felt her face warm. "Oh."

A smile spread slowly across his face as he slipped his arm around her and turned to greet the next person. She hadn't thought beyond the wedding, and now the nerves in her stomach were doing a jig. If she made it through this day, it would be a miracle.

Addison grew rigid at the mention of them being alone together. Her reaction was unexpected and caught him off-guard. Surely, they shared a mutual attraction, didn't they? Maybe she found him unattractive. No, it couldn't be that, or she wouldn't have agreed to marry him, would she have? Maybe the money was the real temptation. It would be for most anyone. Even her. She was only human. Disappointment settled in the pit of his stomach.

He forced a smile as he turned to his mother. "Thanks for all you did, Mom. Everything is perfect."

"I hope it suited Addison's taste. We had to scour her Fractal posts and her Instagram account to get an idea of her tastes and preferences. It would've been much better if she could've been here."

His bride kept her smile pasted in place. "With so little time for the engagement, I couldn't get away, but I would've preferred being here. This island is the most beautiful place

I've ever seen. I can't imagine what I would've done differently."

"Everything was exquisite, wasn't it?" His mother asked.

"It was. Thank you." Addison hugged his mother, and they both had tears in their eyes. He hoped they were happy tears. It was another thing he didn't understand about women, but if they were happy tears, then he'd misread her earlier reaction. There was hope.

Amy approached, and he grinned. "Thanks, Ames."

Her smile was genuine. "Let's never let it happen again, okay?"

"One and done. I promise."

She turned to his bride. "It's nice to meet you. Keep this one in line." She poked Zach in the chest with her index finger. "He's difficult to control."

Addison's face showed her bewilderment. "Addison, this is my assistant, Amy. She's the friend I told you about. She planned the entire wedding, the travel arrangements, the cruise, and every other minute detail all while enduring my mother's constant interference."

"In that case, I can't thank you enough, Amy." She smiled and reached out to shake hands, but Amy pulled her into a hug.

When Amy was safely out of hearing distance, he leaned down and whispered in her ear, "I should've warned you about Amy's exuberance."

"It's fine. She seems great. Although, I must admit, I didn't expect your assistant to be so much better looking than your wife."

"That's not true." He smiled. "Amy is cute in a sisterly way. My bride is gorgeous."

"If you say so."

Addison was grateful when the reception line fizzled out. The photographer pulled them aside for photos while the guests mingled. Her stomach growled as she worked to school her features into those of an adoring bride. It would've been wise to listen to her mother's advice that morning, but no, she'd expected this whole affair to be over in an hour and hadn't considered that she might not have another chance to eat.

After the third time the photographer had her jump in the waves while holding her wedding dress up, she'd had enough. She sent Zach a pleading look.

"Is that enough photos, love?"

Love. Ha! That was a joke. "I like it better when you call me by name."

"Not into terms of endearment, darling?"

"I'd prefer you call me Addison."

"Yes, dear." He grinned, and she punched him playfully in the arm. The photographer got the shot, and she shook her head.

Zach walked over to the photographer and spoke a few words. The man made himself scarce. Before she knew it, Zach was dragging her to the buffet table set up about twenty feet from the makeshift dance floor. "You shouldn't let me know when something irks you. I won't be able to resist doing it, darling."

Before they could partake of the delicious-looking food, a voice came over the sound system, and someone instructed them to make their way to the floor for their first dance as husband and wife. Zach guided her with a hand at the small of her back before sweeping her into his arms. She breathed in the masculine scent of spicy cologne. Smiling up at him, she relaxed into the dance and followed his lead. As exhausted as she was, she still reveled in his nearness. She only hoped she could make it through this day. Too much excitement and not enough sustenance was wearing her thin.

Zach shouldn't have been surprised how perfectly Addison fit in his arms. He'd danced with her the night before, though it felt like it had been weeks ago. Something between them changed with those vows. He couldn't explain it to himself, but everything was different. Now she wasn't his buddy, she was his partner. For life. He sent up a silent prayer. It would've been wiser to pray before the ceremony. Thinking back over the last few months, he swayed to the music. Where had God been in his thoughts? In his actions?

The frequency of his prayers had dwindled down to an unhealthy level since he and Nikki had split-up. Was he angry with God? No. It wasn't anger. It was guilt. God didn't condone premarital sex, but yet he'd allowed himself to partake in the sin without thinking through the consequences. What was done was done. He was a married man now, so it wouldn't happen again. Forcing the thoughts from his mind, he focused on his bride. "I can't imagine a more beautiful bride."

"I bet you say that to all your brides."

"I like your sense of humor." He dipped her, and she grinned up at him.

"A good thing since you're stuck with me now."

When the music stopped, they made their way off the floor, but something was off. Her face turned as white as her dress. "Addison?" Before he could do anything, she was falling. He got behind her, caught her, and gently set her down on the edge of the dance floor. "Addison?" he shouted. Amy pushed through the crowd. She was certified in CPR and as a former EMT she was the closest thing they had to a medical professional on the island. Why hadn't he thought of that? There should've been a doctor on staff.

Her eyes flew opened, and she tried to sit up, but he held her in place.

Her mother hovered nearby. "I told to you to eat."

"Your 'I told you so' isn't helping, Mom," Addison said weakly.

"Is that all that's wrong? You haven't eaten."

Amy gave him a thumbs up. "I'll go make her a plate and get her some orange juice."

"People with low blood sugar can't go without food, Addison."

"Mom. Stop." She put her hands over her face. "I'm already mortified. Please don't make it worse."

Her mother's face reddened, and Zach patted her arm. "I didn't know she had low blood sugar, or I would've made sure she'd eaten."

"She has a handle on it most days, but today she was too nervous to eat."

"And then I didn't make sure she had the opportunity after the ceremony."

"This isn't your fault, Zachary."

"I'm right here, people. Please stop talking about me as if I wasn't." She tried to rise to her feet.

He held her hand, effectively keeping her in place. "Wait here until you've had some orange juice at least."

"Fine."

After a glass of orange juice and a few bites of food, the color returned to her cheeks, and he breathed a sigh of relief.

Zach's feet were sore, but he couldn't deny Amy when she requested the next dance. He'd gotten his bride on the floor for several dances before dancing with his mother and her mother, so it was time for him to spread the love.

"You seem happy." She tilted her head to the side.

He grinned. "Did you expect me to be unhappy on my wedding day?"

"Don't flash those dimples at me." She narrowed her eyes. "I'm not sure what I expected. I kind of figured this was one of those prearranged 'let's get married if we're still single' things, so I didn't expect you to be this ecstatic about it."

"How could you possibly know that?" he choked on the words. Maybe she'd seen the emails. He hoped she wouldn't mention it to anyone as it could cause his new wife embarrassment if anyone knew why they'd married.

She slapped his back and grinned. "I'm your right-hand girl, so I'm forced to know how to read you. You've been expecting me to read your mind for the last five years."

"Oh."

"That doesn't sound like a denial. Are you confirming my suspicions?"

"Yeah. I guess." He grimaced. "Keep it to yourself, Ames."

"Mums the word." She sighed wistfully. "What is it about this girl that makes you willing to give up every other woman on the planet?"

"I'm not sure I have a straight answer for that." He spun her around once and brought her back to him.

"Figure it out soon. At some point, she'll ask. You'd do well to have an answer when she does."

"Ames, Addison knows what this marriage is about, and she's happy with the parameters. She doesn't expect a declaration of my undying love. We're both ready to settle down and start a family with someone we can trust. We can have that with each other."

"The new Mrs. Williams might not ask today, but she will in time. She's a woman. We have an innate need to understand our relationships." The song ended, and Amy kissed him on the cheek. "She got herself a wonderful man. I won't pretend I'm not a tad bit jealous. I hope she appreciates you."

"I got a fabulous woman in Addison." He smiled. "I've never felt more blessed, and when you give your heart to a man, I know he'll be a better man than I."

"That's obvious." She giggled and took a step back. "Don't forget what I said."

As he watched Amy make her way back to the house, he stood alone and contemplated her words. Maybe she was right, and Addison would want more than he was willing to give.

Lucy Williams was headed toward Addison at full speed, so she braced herself for the conversation to come. Her mother-in-law draped an arm around her shoulder and steered her away from the crowd of people about to board the cruise ship. She hoped this wouldn't take long since she wanted a moment to say goodbye to her mother and apologize for her earlier behavior.

Mrs. Williams let go of Addison and took a step back. "Welcome to the family, dear."

"Thank you, Mrs. Williams."

"Call me 'Mom,' dear."

"Thank you. I will."

"Take care of my son." She had tears pooling in her eyes.

Addison embraced her and patted her back. "I plan to. I can promise you that."

"He doesn't know what a huge step the two of you took today, but it won't be long before the realization hits him." She blinked rapidly. "When it does, you need to be strong enough for both of you."

"I'll try." She frowned. "This marriage business is scary, but together Zach and I can make it work. At least that's what I keep telling myself."

"Keep that attitude, and you'll be fine." She turned back toward the crowd. "I'll let you say your goodbyes to the cruise people."

Addison meandered back to her mother while Mrs. Williams walked up ahead of her.

"Where have you been, dear? We thought we would have to leave without saying goodbye." Her mother pulled her by the arm over to meet her gentleman friend. "This is Christopher. He's one of your husband's chefs." She leaned up closer to Addison's ear and whispered, "and a fantastic dancer."

"It's a pleasure to meet you, Christopher." She extended her hand.

He shook her hand. "And you."

"Will you be going on the cruise?"

"I will." There was a sparkle in the man's eyes. He clearly found her mother fascinating.

Her mother hooked her arm through hers and took a few steps away. "What do you think?"

"I think you're a grown woman and if you like Christopher, then you should enjoy the time you get to spend together before you both go back to your real lives."

"You don't think we can make it work?"

"I think it's a little early to be picking out rings, but I would be one to talk, wouldn't I?"

Her mother laughed. "Go find your husband. I'll see you after the cruise. Zachary promised to fly you home for a visit or fly us out to see you. He said it was up to you."

"I know which one you'll pick. I'll see you in California, Mom."

Addison found Zach, and they stood side by side and said goodbye to their guests as they boarded the ship. She couldn't believe so many people attended her wedding reception when she'd only invited her mother to join her on the island. She was grateful her mother had thought to include Parker. Otherwise, it would've only been her mother on her side. Zachary had a huge staff of people, and they'd all seemed genuinely happy for them.

Once everyone had boarded the ship except for the few remaining guests who were taking the jet, Addison and Zach stood with Mrs. Williams, Parker, and Amy, and waved at everyone lined up on the deck of the ship.

Addison glanced up from her cake and spotted her sister making her way toward their table. "I'll be back, Zach." She stood to greet Parker as she arrived at the table. "Want to take a walk down the beach?"

"Yeah. I'd like that." Parker kicked off her shoes and placed them under the table.

They'd walked nearly a quarter mile down the beach before Parker spoke. "I am happy for you."

"Thank you."

"I'm not sure why you married Zach on a dare or a pact or whatever it was, but I always liked him. You two will make ideal partners. I'm convinced of it."

"What's bothering you, Parker?"

"Ben."

"What about him?"

"I love him, but I feel guilty about it. I know that you and I can't have a normal relationship if we don't talk about what happened in high school."

"Sweetie, I've been over Ben for a long time."

"I know. I do. I know that. It's just that, well..."

"Spit it out." Addison looked out over the calm ocean which was such a contrast with her sister's tumultuous spirit.

"I'm not."

"What aren't you over? I didn't steal Ben from you."

"I'm not over hurting you."

"I was the maid of honor at your wedding, Parker. How can you not be over it?"

"The guilt is killing me."

"I forgive you. I forgave you a long time ago."

"So, why is it bothering me so much?"

"I don't know. Maybe it has more to do with getting right with God and less to do with me than you think."

She let out a harsh laugh. "I don't have a thing to say to God."

"Well, until that changes, you will not find happiness, let alone joy."

"You religious people are all the same. God is the answer to everything."

"He is."

Parker dug in the sand with her toes. "Let's head back."

"Okay." Addison hoped that her words would plant a seed. Her sister wasn't ready to turn to God, but someday this conversation might come to mind.

Zach and Addison stood beside the jet as his mother, her sister, and Amy boarded. They were the last remaining guests on the island. Zach thought Amy's idea for sending the guests and staff on a cruise was ingenious, since it allowed him and his bride to honeymoon here on the island with no interruptions. He'd given his employees the week off. It served two purposes, engendering good will among the staff and giving him some much-needed time alone with his wife. It was a win-win.

He put his arm around Addison's shoulders and steered her away from the plane. "We don't want to be standing this close when they take off."

She rubbed the back of her neck.

"Sore?"

"A little. I think yesterday's quad ride gave me whiplash."

"Are you suggesting I'm a bad driver?"

"Yes." She laughed. The sound of her laughter reminded him of the lazy days they'd spent together on the beach.

"You still up for zip lining?"

"I never said I was up for it. What I said was that I'd do it."

"Close enough. Let's go change."

"Aren't you exhausted after the wedding?"

"Maybe you should rest first. We have a couple of hours of daylight left."

"No. It's fine." She followed him into the house, and when they got to the hallway, she headed down the east wing toward her room.

"Where are you going?"

"To get changed."

"Your room is over here now."

She turned to face him but didn't meet his gaze. "I didn't think of that. I need to get my stuff though."

"Your things are in our room."

She froze.

He closed the distance between them. "Are you afraid of me, Addison?"

She stood stock still staring at the floor, not answering.

"You are." He took a step back and rocked on his heels, crossing his arms over his chest. "This morning I couldn't decide if you were afraid of me or repulsed by me. Now I can see that it's fear."

She raised her gaze to meet his. "Repulsed? Where is that coming from?"

"Your reaction earlier. Never mind that. It obviously wasn't accurate. It's fright. I'm sure of it now. You're terrified. I can't believe Addison Scott is afraid of me, her closest friend in the world."

"We haven't been close in a long time, Zach."

"What's changed? We're the same two people."

"We've both changed."

"What matters hasn't changed."

"How can you possibly know that?"

"I can see right through you. You're the same sweet girl."

"I'm not a girl anymore."

"No. You aren't." He smiled uncertainly. "But you are my girl, right?"

She giggled. "I suppose I am."

"Then, will you please come to our room?" He took her hand, and they walked together toward the master suite. When they got to the doorway, he swept her up into his arms.

"What are you doing?!"

"I'm carrying you across the threshold."

She swatted at his chest, and he chuckled. He set her down inside the room and allowed himself a moment to admire the fit of her wedding gown. When his gaze traveled up to her face, he saw terror in her eyes. It was too much.

"I promise not to hurt you, Addison."

"We've been through this. I know you won't hurt me."

"Then what is it?"

"I don't have a lot of experience, and I feel like we're rushing into this."

"We're married."

"I know."

His lips pressed together in a tight line. "If you're not ready, we'll wait."

"You're willing to wait?"

"It's not what I want, but I'd prefer that you were comfortable sharing my bed. You can sleep in here, and I'll stay in another room until you're ready." He knew his smile was hard, but he could not soften it.

She wrapped her arms around her middle and sat on the edge of the bed. "I don't want to throw you out of your own bedroom. I was comfortable in the other room."

"This is *our* room. I want you to be comfortable here. You're my wife. It's better this way."

"If it's what you want."

A hard laugh escaped. "What I want is to throw you down on that bed and have my way with you, but I'll settle for a few stolen kisses until you're eager for more." His head bent to hers, and he gently brushed his lips across hers keeping a tight control on his churning emotions. "You never have to be afraid of me, Addison. I'll never push you into anything you're not ready for." Then he turned away and gathered some of his clothes before making a hasty exit.

Chapter 6

Addison stood alone in the enormous master bedroom with her fingers on her lips wishing the kiss had lasted longer. It was asking too much for them to wait to be intimate. She knew it before the words came out but couldn't stop them. It was a request that should've been made before they'd said their vows.

They were married now, so there wasn't anything wrong with them sleeping together, but for her it seemed too soon. She'd been faithful to her vow to save herself for marriage, but now that the time came, she couldn't give herself to him. The 'what ifs' flooded her mind. What if she gave him everything only to fall short of his expectations, would he divorce her? He couldn't know about her inexperience, but it would soon become obvious. She couldn't live up to the women he'd been with. His exploits with supermodels and actresses were public knowledge. What had she been thinking agreeing to marry him without talking to him about it first? She didn't want to be one more in his long line of conquests when he would be her first and, God willing, her last. Why had he chosen to marry her? She wouldn't be his first, but he chose her for a reason. It would have to be enough. She sat on the edge of the bed and let the tears overcome her.

When she calmed down, she changed out of her wedding dress with shaking fingers and put on shorts and a fitted t-shirt. She found him on the patio staring out over the ocean. He was wearing his glasses. Upon reaching his side, she put her hand on his back, but he stiffened in response, so she withdrew. "I didn't know you still wore your glasses. Thought you must've had that laser eye surgery."

"Not yet. Most of the time I wear contacts. They were bothering my eyes, so I took them out."

"It's a great look."

He continued staring out over the waves instead of turning to face her.

"If you still want to do this, we should get going. I don't think we have much time left for this zip lining adventure you planned. The sun won't wait for us."

"I would've made sure we didn't have time for it if you'd have encouraged me to stay."

She hesitated, unsure how to respond. "I'm sorry, Zach." She closed the distance between them and raised a hand to his face. "I truly am sorry." For a moment, she could see the pain in his eyes.

"I won't pretend to understand what this is about, but I'll give you the space you need." His mask went back up, and a big goofy grin replaced the hurt she'd seen on his face only seconds earlier. "Race me to the quad. We're taking that zip line whether or not the sun goes down."

"Where is it?" He pointed, and she ran to the beach where he'd left the ATV. She hopped on in front of him. "I'm driving."

"I'm not sure I like the sound of that. You don't know your way around the island."

"I remember how to get to the tree house."

"Oh, boy."

He climbed onto the quad behind her. She glanced back when she didn't feel his arms around her waist and saw he'd chosen to hold on to the metal rack behind him instead of her. Maybe he thought it would be safer. Either that, or he was still upset. There was no telling which it was. His spicy cologne assaulted her senses before the smell of fuel replaced it as she took off down the beach.

"Hey, slow down. You'll throw me off." He hollered over the engine noise.

She laughed and sped up. "Payback."

They were both laughing when they pulled up outside of the tree house. "You ready to fly like a bird, darling?"

"Cut that out."

"What's that, love?"

She growled, and he laughed. After opening the shed, he removed some kind of harness and helped her put it on. His touch felt intimate as he strapped her into the contraption, and his slow, methodical movements made it crystal clear that he was enjoying her discomfort. He attached his own harness and pointed to the rope ladder. Taking the hint, she climbed up and headed out to the deck to wait for him there. Coming up behind her, he put his hands on her shoulders. "This will be fun."

"If you say so." She fidgeted with her rings.

"Come on." He hooked her to the zip line. "Tell me when you're ready."

She bit her bottom lip. "If you wait for me to give you the okay, I may never go." Seconds later she was flying above the tree line enjoying the feeling of freedom. When she reached the end of the line, there was a wooden landing. She got her feet under her and unclipped herself, leaning on the rail for support. She couldn't stop beaming. What a rush.

He arrived thirty seconds later. "Awe-inspiring, isn't it?" He unclipped himself and turned around in a circle with his arms in the air.

"I'm glad we didn't do this in the dark. The view is breathtaking. I wouldn't have wanted to miss it."

He stared into her eyes. "The view is exceptional."

Every nerve ending in her body was suddenly electrified. She broke eye contact. "The view of the waterfall was amazing"

He stepped out of his harness. "I thought you'd enjoy seeing it from above."

"I did." She followed suit and removed her gear.

He reached for her hand. "You're shaking. It's the adrenaline. Give it a few minutes to wear off before taking the stairs. They're steep."

She sat on the bench built into the landing deck. "I guess that's what the seat is here for."

"You know it."

"Thank you for suggesting this. I had a blast."

"I'm glad." He squeezed her hand. "We'll have loads of fun together, Addison."

She grinned up at him. "I'm glad we did this."

"The zip lining or the marriage."

"Both, but I meant the marriage."

"Are you sure about that?" He bent down close to her, his lips inches from hers. "I got an entirely contradictory vibe this morning."

"I apologize if I ruined our wedding day."

"Nothing is ruined." His lips touched hers briefly. She wanted to prolong the kiss but didn't have the courage to pull him back to her. So, when he rose to his feet, she did the same. "Ready?"

"Sure." Only now she was shaking again for reasons having little to do with zip lining.

A platonic marriage wasn't what he'd signed up for, but he was a patient man. If she wanted to wait, they'd wait. He took the steps slowly, so Addison wouldn't rush. He didn't need her falling to her death. The thought made his throat constrict. It should've been a longer engagement. Why had he hurried the wedding along? Now that they were married, it was evident he'd sped it along for no good reason, but two weeks ago it had seemed like a splendid idea.

Nikki. The answer came to him, and he felt shame. He'd rushed the wedding because of his ex-fiancée. He'd, mistakenly, thought it would get her off his back. Instead, she'd flown into a rage when the news of his wedding plans reached her. She'd shown up at his office, eyes flashing with insanity, and demanded he call off the wedding. He'd ducked in time to avoid the caramel macchiato she'd thrown at him, but the look in her eyes haunted him. He'd come so close to marrying her, and now as he looked at Addison, he realized how blessed he was to not have said 'I do' to the wrong woman. He started the trek back to the tree house, and she fell in step beside him.

"Where to now?"

"We have a bit of a walk to get back to the quad."

"We didn't go far."

"It's a lot farther than it felt."

"I'm glad I wore my hiking boots."

"Stay close. The rain forest can be dangerous at dusk. You might not see snakes or other dangers."

"I didn't think of that."

"I'll protect you." Slipping an arm around her shoulders, he considered stopping to kiss her, but the need to get out of the forest was more pressing. It wasn't as if she was ready for the intimacy anyway, and though he'd joked about taking her zip lining in the dark, he hadn't been serious. The dangers lurking in the forest at night were too great a risk to subject his bride to them.

She stopped in her tracks and looked up at him, her hands on her hips. "You'd better."

"Better what?" He'd forgotten what they'd been talking about.

"Protect me."

"Or what?"

"Or else."

"Or else what?"

"I don't know yet."

"You've grown feisty in your old age, darling."

"Enough with the darling, and who are you calling old?"

He chuckled and resumed the hike.

She was breathing heavily when they reached the tree house. Flopping to the ground, she grinned up at him.

"I should've told you to pack a bag, then we could've stayed the night instead of riding back to the main house."

"I wouldn't want to intrude on your private space."

"Well, that's too bad." He turned away from her but looked back over his shoulder. "I would welcome the intrusion."

He hopped on the quad before she got any ideas about driving again. It wasn't a good idea for her to navigate the path in the dark and the sun was nearly gone. When she mounted the quad behind him, her arms slipped around his waist and he felt his muscles tighten at the touch of her fingers. He had to get a grip before he pushed her too far. If she wasn't ready, he needed to respect that. The effect she had on him wasn't making it easy though. If he gave in and kissed her with the passion he wanted to, he'd scare her further into her shell. After turning the headlights on, he drove them back to the house.

They arrived back at the house, and Zach pulled the quad into a garage filled with equipment and toys. She looked around at the boats, dirt bikes, and quads. "What's all this for?" Addison jumped off the quad and stood beside it.

"Mostly for fun."

"I figured that, but you can't ride it all."

"Sometimes I have guests."

"You must have a lot of them."

He laughed. "Let's get some dinner."

"Who's cooking? You sent the staff away, remember?"

"Greta prepared everything we'll need. All we have to do is heat it up."

"Nice." She grinned. "I'm liking Greta a great deal, and I don't think I even met her."

"You met her this morning, but you can't be expected to remember everyone. It was a hectic morning."

"Great. When people ask me to describe my wedding day, I can say it was 'hectic.'"

"It was, but I hope you'll also think of it as magical."

"It was."

"I'm glad. I hoped it would be."

She stood on her tiptoes and placed an experimental kiss on his lips. After a sharp intake of breath he pulled away. His hasty retreat concerned her. Had she messed up again?

He hurried to the back door, and she followed him into the kitchen. Zach heated the food while she gathered up plates and silverware to set the table. He suggested she set the table on the patio, so they could eat while watching the waves lap at the shore. When he brought the food out, she said grace silently before they ate their reheated meal. He left momentarily and returned with chocolate mousse for dessert.

"I shouldn't." She stared at the sweet dish.

"Why not?"

"I'm supposed to keep my sugar levels even rather than binge on junk. Protein takes longer to break down, so it's my go-to choice, although a bite or two of sweets won't hurt me. This looks scrumptious."

He put it in front of her with a spoon. "Don't pass out on me again. I'm not sure my heart can take the stress."

She took a bite. "I promise to be careful."

Once she'd had a taste, she set her spoon down and walked to the water's edge. She felt Zach watching her as she waded into the water.

A few minutes later, he was beside her. "It's been a long day. You should get some rest."

"I am tired." She kicked at the water. "The water is so warm. Nothing like the Delaware and Maryland beaches, huh?"

"Nothing like it, but those days and nights on the beach with you were some of the best times of my life."

"Mine too."

"Come on. Let's go in." He reached for her hand, but she scurried away and kicked water in his direction.

He wiped salt water from his face. "You will pay for that you little minx." Reaching down, he used both hands to splash her.

She collapsed in a fit of giggles, so he reached out to help her up, but he didn't release her. Instead, he tugged her close and held her firmly against him. Every fiber in her body responded to him, but soon after he initiated the contact, he broke the spell by dropping his hands and taking a step back. She longed to tell him how much she'd wanted his kiss, but her courage failed, and the words didn't come.

When he reached the dry sand, he called back to her. "Let's get inside."

Chapter 7

Addison lay awake for hours rolling around in the giant bed. In the wee hours of the morning sleep caught up with her, but a pounding on the bedroom door interrupted her slumber. She pulled a pillow over her face, but the pounding didn't stop.

Rising from the bed she stomped her way to the door and threw it open. "What?" she growled.

Zach stood there grinning. "Not a morning person, sunshine?"

"What do you want?"

"To take you kayaking." She was disappointed that his glasses were gone.

"Kayaking?"

"That's what I said."

She looked down at her crumpled t-shirt and gym shorts. "Let me get dressed."

"I'll wait in the kitchen. You will eat before we go."

"Bossy, aren't you?" She put her hands on her hips. "What if I'm not hungry?"

"Tough. You're eating breakfast."

He turned to go, and she hurried into the bathroom. When she glimpsed herself in the mirror, she cringed. She'd answered the door with her hair flying in every direction. Taking her time, she showered and dressed so she would be presentable. It wasn't as if the kayaks would float away before they got to them.

When she arrived in the kitchen, Zach had her plate filled with eggs, pancakes, and sausage. She stared at the food. "You can't expect me to eat this much food."

"Eat as much or as little as you like." He smirked. "I rifled through the cabinets and found sugar-free syrup since you said you're not supposed to OD on sugar."

She narrowed her eyes. "If you think I'm using sugar-free anything you have another thing coming. Do you have strawberries or bananas and whipped cream?"

"Yeah. I think so."

Raiding the refrigerator, she pulled out what she needed and cut up the strawberries. When she reached the table, Zach was waiting for her and hadn't touched his food.

"What are you waiting for?"

"Don't you want to say grace?"

"Right. Sorry."

"Don't be. I noticed you prayed over your food last night. I would've said grace out loud, but I'm not used to sharing a meal with another Christian. It's nice."

She bowed her head, and he led them in prayer thanking the Lord for the bounty He'd provided. When she met his eyes, she couldn't help but smile. She'd never been around a man who prayed out loud, and it surprised her how attractive she found him in that moment.

Addison devoured her food. She hadn't realized how hungry she was.

"I guess you can eat more than you thought." He grinned showing off both dimples.

"Yeah. Maybe so." She returned his smile. "It's a good thing we'll be kayaking, so I can work off the calories."

"You needed the sustenance. You've been going nonstop for days."

"Whose fault is that?" She laughed.

"I plead the fifth." He went to the sink to wash up the dishes, and she rummaged through the drawers until she found a dish towel, and then dried.

"You see the dishwasher there, right?" she asked.

"It's easier to hand wash them."

"If you say so."

"It's not like I get to do dishes often."

She grinned. "If you expect me to feel sorry for you because your help doesn't let you do dishes, you can forget it."

"I guess that came out wrong."

"Yeah. Made you sound like an over-privileged brat."

"You know better." He took the towel from her hand. "There is no church on the island, but if you need time for your morning devotions and Bible reading before we go, I'll understand completely."

"It can wait until we get back. What about you?"

"I start all my mornings with God's word. Today was no exception."

"In that case, I'll definitely wait until after our excursion."

"In that case, let's head out to the boat launch on the lake. From there it's only a few feet to the creek."

"Creek? We're not kayaking in the ocean?"

"We can if you're confident in your abilities. The sea kayaks are in the garage, but I think you'll prefer the stream. It should be calm and serene."

"Sounds fantastic."

"Let's take the ATV."

"You take that quad everywhere, huh?"

"We could take a dirt bike if you'd prefer?"

"Let's stick with the quad."

"Single or tandem?"

"What do you mean?"

"Do you want to kayak by yourself or with me? I need to know which kayak or kayaks to untie."

"I haven't done this before, so tandem might be best."

"A first-timer." Zach untied a bright green kayak. He instructed her on how to hold the paddle before he put the vessel in the water and held it still for her. "You'll sit up front."

He climbed in behind her. "That's it but use your torso to power the movement instead of relying on your arm strength. Now loosen your grip. If you hold it that tightly we won't make it far before your hands give out."

She relaxed a little, and they sliced through the water. A short time later, they were in the midst of the rain forest. It didn't take long for her to feel like she'd been paddling for hours. Zach stopped paddling and suggested she do the same. Then, he tossed her a bottle of water.

She caught it and took a swig. "Thanks. You didn't mention the stream came through the rain forest."

"It's a tiny island. Everything goes through the rain forest."

"A few days ago I'd never seen one. Now, it almost feels like home. It's so peaceful here."

"It is home. A vacation home, but it's one of our homes."

"That sounds so outrageous. Who ever thought we'd have more than one home?"

"Not me." He chuckled.

"I can feel the awesome presence of God in this place. His artistry is evident everywhere I turn."

"Hence the reason I purchased the island." The winds picked up and leaves fell into the surrounding water. "We'd better head back. It feels like a storm's brewing."

"The remnants of that hurricane you mentioned the other day?"

"No. There wouldn't be remnants yet, it isn't expected to make landfall until this evening. It should miss us completely. Just to be certain, we'll check the radar when we get back."

"What about the cruise ship?" Her brow wrinkled in concern. "Will my mother and the others be in danger?"

"I spoke with the captain before they left, he was heading the ship toward Cancun, and they expect the storm to veer north barely skimming the Bahamas on its way to make landfall in Port St. Lucie, Florida. Even if it changes course, the ship moves far faster than the storm and can easily outrun it."

Another few minutes passed. "We should head back. I know you're not used to paddling, and could use a longer break, but we should return to the house."

When they arrived back at the boat launch, she rubbed her tired arms. "I will be sore tomorrow."

"I'm sorry I pushed you so hard." His brow crinkled, and his eyes filled with concern.

"Is there something you're not telling me?"

"No. It's just... never mind. Let's get back and look at the radar."

He hopped onto the quad and she followed suit holding onto his waist. Zach made haste back toward the main house.

He'd barely stopped the ATV before he was running to the door.

"You're keeping something from me."

The wind picked up, and she heard the shutters banging.

He rubbed his brow. "The hurricane is coming. I feel it. It's not supposed to hit us, but I think it must've veered this way. I should've double-checked before we left the house this morning."

"We're stuck on this island in a hurricane?" She gnawed on her bottom lip.

"Let's check the radar and see what the experts are saying. My gut instinct could be wrong."

She gave him a skeptical look as the lights flickered when they entered the kitchen.

"Don't worry we have an emergency generator."

"It's not the power I'm worried about." She twisted her rings.

He hurried to his office, opened the door, and sat down at his desk, surrounded by half a dozen computer monitors. "We're safe here. I'll keep you safe."

"Okay." She glanced around the room, eyes widening. "You didn't show me this room during the tour."

"I rarely share it. Like the tree house, it's my space. Completely, as in I let no one in it, except you now that you're my wife. Nobody can come in here. Not even to clean. It must stay locked at all times. Same with my home and work offices in California." He raked his fingers through his hair. "It'll take a moment to get these back up and running after that power blip."

"Why so much secrecy?"

"Company secrets."

"The infamous Fractal algorithms?"

"Among other things."

"We're powered up. Let me see here." He focused on the screen as he opened the NOAA website. "The good news is that Florida may be spared a direct hit, but the bad news is we're getting it instead. We only have a few hours to prepare."

"You loaded that website quick. I think you have better internet here than I have at home."

"The fiber optics cost an arm and a leg, but it's worth it for me considering my profession. We don't have time to chat about connection speeds though. How are you with a screw gun?"

"Terrible. I thought you said we were safe here."

"We will be once we board up the windows."

"Do we have what we need for that?"

"I'm a boy scout. Always prepared."

"You forget who you're talking to. You were never a boy scout. Show me how to work the screw gun, and I'll help you."

He got a screw gun from the garage and carried out the plywood two boards at a time. He kept it on hand for storm preparations, but this would be the first time he needed to board the place up himself. Considering he'd sent the staff away; it was the only option available. Once he had boards set out around the house, he set the torque on the screw gun and showed Addison how to use it. Then he set up two ladders side by side, it wasn't an ideal way to accomplish the task, but they didn't have a lot of time to do things properly. He held the boards while she screwed them in. He hadn't planned to spend their honeymoon on storm prep, but at least his bride wasn't whining like a child. He thought about Nikki and a deep sigh escaped.

"What was that for?" She stopped what she was doing, glared at him, and cleared her throat.

"What was what for?"

"That exasperated sigh. I'm doing my best. I don't need the attitude."

"It had nothing to do with you."

"Sure, it didn't."

He groaned. "I was thinking of someone else."

"Whatever."

"I was wrong anyway." His words had a bite.

"About?"

"I was thinking how different you were from Nikki. How she'd be acting like a child. I guess you aren't so different."

"So, now I'm a child?" She climbed down the ladder. "Wait one minute, Zachary. Who is Nikki and how did she enter this conversation?"

"Nikki is my ex-fiancée."

"You were planning to marry someone else?" She set the screw gun on the top of the ladder with a little too much force, and her eyes flashed. "This didn't seem worth mentioning before the wedding?"

"I thought you knew. It was public knowledge."

"It might come as a surprise to you, mister big shot, but not everyone follows the news of your exploits in the media. I had a life of my own."

"I didn't mean it like that." He approached her, but she turned away from him. He spoke to her back. "Please, Addison, I apologize, but we need to get this done. If we don't, we won't have a safe place to ride out the storm." He glanced out over the ocean at the waves now beating the shoreline with a force he'd never seen on the tiny cay.

She turned to face him. "We'll continue this conversation after we finish getting the house ready." She climbed the ladder and looked down at him. "You're not off-the-hook yet."

"Thank you for helping." He forced a smile. "You're the best."

"Don't suck up. I'm a long way from forgiving you."

They sat on opposite sides of the room. He played with his weather radio while she played a game of solitaire.

"The house has been through hurricanes before. It's only a category two, so it shouldn't be too terrible."

"The ocean could swallow up the whole island."

"It's not a tsunami, sweetie."

"My name is Addison."

"I'm sorry. Let's talk about this thing between us, okay?"

"I'm not ready to talk."

"Please, Addy."

A tear slid down her cheek, and he had enough. He took her hands and pulled her out of the chair. "Talk to me. I can't take this."

She tugged her hands free from him. "Why didn't you tell me about this Nikki girl? How long ago did the two of you break-up?"

"The answer will sound bad."

"How long?"

"About two months ago."

"I'm the rebound girl. You married your rebound."

"That's not fair. You know I don't think of you that way."

"I know nothing about you, Zach. We haven't spoken since high school except the occasional email or social media posts."

"Would you believe me if I said I don't have feelings for her anymore?"

"No."

"I caught her with Greg. He was my lawyer. They were fooling around in my conference room."

Her face was streaked with tears. "It's still not all right that you didn't tell me about her."

He didn't know how to make the situation better. He'd hurt her, and he was at a loss for how to fix it. "I didn't think she was important." Once again, he tried to touch her, but she pulled away and stalked across the room.

"How can I make things better?"

"You can't fix this. I need time."

He groaned. "Whatever you need. If you want time, I'll give you time." The wind whistled louder, and the lights flickered again. He rose to his feet and ambled over to where she sat. "I know I should've told you. I'm sorry."

A loud bang made her jump before the house went dark. "That was probably the power station." He rummaged in a cabinet for some candles, lit one, and placed it on a table nearby. Then he held his arms open, fearful of further rejection, but wanting to offer Addison comfort as the storm bore down on them. He could see her reluctance, but she came to him and he held her near, not wanting the storm to end for fear she would no longer need him. "The lights should come back on soon if the generator kicks on as it's designed to do." He placed a kiss on the top of her head and guided her over to the couch. "If this gets much worse, we might need to use the storm shelter."

She sat up straight and met his gaze. "You have one, and we're not using it?"

"I hoped we wouldn't need it." He pointed to an area rug. "There are steps under there."

She hurried to the rug and pulled it out of the way. "I think we should go down there now."

He bent down beside her, unhooked the latch, released the stairs, and then walked back over to blow out the candle. "After you, my dear."

"Shouldn't you go first?" She didn't complain about his use of an endearment, so he knew she must be terrified.

"No. I have to put the stairs back and close the latch to keep the storm from being able to pull us out of the shelter."

"You're not making me feel any safer."

Chapter 8

The hours ticked by slowly as she stared at the ceiling of the storm shelter. "This space is too small. I'm getting claustrophobic."

"You're the one who wanted to come down here."

"Fine. Blame me. You're the one who built it this small."

"Are you nearly through berating me?"

She closed her eyes and clenched her fists. Was she being unfair? Was it unreasonable to expect that he would disclose his previous engagement before they married? She didn't think so, but it wouldn't help their marriage for her to stay angry. "I'm sorry. I may be blowing this out of proportion, but I need some time to get over it, okay?"

"It wasn't intentional, Addison. Maybe I should've known to mention her, but I didn't. The omission wasn't meant to cause you pain."

Was that what she was feeling, pain? Yes. It hurt, but if she was completely honest, what she felt was envy. He'd chosen the other woman first. If his ex-fiancée hadn't messed up, Addison wouldn't be here now with these rings on her finger. She had no right to be envious when they hadn't spoken in years. It wasn't as if she'd had a claim on him. Even now, she refused to let him touch her. Despite all that, she was the one sulking. How must he feel?

"You should've told me, but I know I'm overreacting. I can't seem to help it."

"Please sit with me."

She sat up and scooted over to him. His arm wrapped around her automatically, and she found his closeness comforting despite her emotional turmoil.

She hadn't meant to fall asleep, but she awakened to Zach stroking her hair. The sensations his touch provoked were pleasant, so she didn't want him to stop. "How long was I out?"

"About an hour."

She sat up. "I'm sorry."

"Don't be. It's been a hectic week. You must've needed the rest."

"I couldn't sleep last night."

He cocked an eyebrow, but she didn't elaborate. There was no reason to burden him with her fears of inadequacy.

"I'm going upstairs to check the radar to see how much of the storm has passed. Wait down here."

"I want to come up, too."

"I'd prefer you didn't, but if you must, stay in the house. Do not, under any circumstances, venture outside."

She saluted him and followed him up the stairs.

Addison watched as Zach hauled the air-mattress down the stairs into the storm shelter.

She shifted her weight from one foot to the other as he inflated it. "We can't fit two of those down here. Shouldn't we sleep upstairs in our bedrooms?"

"No. We shouldn't. The storm won't be easing up for hours yet, so it's best for us to be down here until it does."

"Are we going to sleep in shifts?"

"No, darling. This mattress is plenty large enough for us to share. I think we've established that I will not force myself on you, so you might as well get a full night's rest."

"Okay." There was no way she'd get any restful sleep with him inches away but arguing over it was pointless.

Zach removed the backpack he'd slung over his shoulder and reached inside, pulling out a worn leather Bible. "I thought you might want this."

"Is this yours?"

"It is, but it's not the one I use every day, so you can keep it if you want."

"Maybe I'll hold on to it for a few days. I left my Bible in Pennsylvania."

They sat together and took turns reading. Addison marveled at how different things were with Zach than they had been with Seth. It hadn't occurred to her that she might marry a man who wanted to read God's word. When the night grew late, Zach extinguished the light and lay beside her on the air-mattress.

She turned away from her groom and stared at the concrete wall. It was quiet in the shelter, so much so she could barely make out the hum of the generator. Every so often, she would hear the wind whistling as the storm continued to pound the tiny cay, but for the most part Zach's steady breathing was the only thing she heard. There was a gulf between them on the mattress, and it seemed like a metaphor for the vast chasm separating them. It was her fault, but she was afraid to take the steps to cross the distance and mend the rift.

Rolling over to face him, she studied his features. To say that he was handsome was an understatement. Any woman in her right mind would be thrilled to trade places with Addison, and none of them would be likely to reject his advances. She wondered if she was too emotionally damaged to be any use as anyone's wife, let alone Zach's. Closing her eyes, she once again attempted to let sleep claim her, and she must've drifted off since the next time she opened her eyes Zach was watching her with those dreamy blue eyes she adored.

Mouthwash would've been nice to have at that moment, so she could kiss her husband good morning without scaring him off.

Zach broke eye contact and got to his feet. "I will see if I can make us some coffee."

"All right." She held the sheet to her chest despite being fully dressed.

"I'll be back in a minute."

"Okay."

A few minutes later he returned with coffee and bagels. "The radar shows the storm is still over us, but nearly half of it has passed."

"Wow. It must be a large storm if it's only half over."

"As long as it doesn't slow down, it should be gone within the next sixteen hours or so."

"I'd like to go upstairs and brush my teeth if you think it's safe."

"It should be fine. I'll come with you."

He could no longer hear the hum of the generator which meant no internet. Since they didn't have a cell tower, his mobile phone wasn't an option. He stood and pushed his chair under the desk with more force than necessary.

It would only take a minute to inspect the house for damage. Leaving Addison at the kitchen table with a glass of water, he moved quickly. So far, only a small amount of water had trickled in under the backdoor. The garage hadn't fared as well. The water was knee high, and the equipment had shifted. There wouldn't be much chance of saving anything.

Three minutes later, he was searching for Addison who'd disappeared on him. After frantically checking the house, he looked outside and spotted her on the beach. His stomach dropped to the floor. Running to the door, he shouted "Addison!"

She was sitting in the sand by the edge of the water, too far away to hear him. The wind and waves were picking up again, but she seemed oblivious.

He ran to her side and fought for control of his racing heart.

She stood to face him.

"Addison, we're in the eye. It isn't over."

As if to punctuate his words, the wind picked up, and she lost her footing. He reached for her arm, but she brushed him away. "I'm fine." She took a few steps.

The wind pulled the roof off a shed near the house and spun it in the air. He grabbed her by the waist, tossed her over his shoulder, and ran toward the house. Once inside, he set her down and pinned her between his body and the back door. "I told you to stay inside!"

"I don't take orders well." The glint in her eyes was defiant.

"Obviously." He was breathing hard.

She sucked in a breath. "You didn't have to manhandle me."

"Were you trying to get yourself killed?"

"It was beautiful when I went outside. The ocean was calm, and the sun was shining."

"You're not a child. You know how hurricanes work. When you're in the storm's eye it's calm, but it doesn't last, and it isn't safe to venture outside."

He could see some of the fire go out of her. She stared sullenly down at the ground.

"Look at me, Addison." She did. "Do you hate me that much that you'd rather get yourself killed than be with me?"

"You know I don't hate you."

"What do you feel for me?"

"I... I... well... um..."

"Never mind. Why don't you show me instead?" He lowered his mouth to hers and kissed her with all the passion he'd been holding back. There was no mistaking her response, she might harbor reservations, but she definitely wasn't frigid. His lips moved to her neck. Her skin tasted like the sea. The reminder of her risking her life and going out by the ocean brought him back to reality. "Don't scare me like that again." His words were spoken quietly, but his irritation couldn't be disguised. He left her standing there and went to his temporary bedroom.

His exit was abrupt, but necessary. He sat on the edge of the bed he hadn't bothered to make. If he was going to keep his promise to give her time, then he had to temper his physical response, and he couldn't do that with her looking at him like a besotted teenager. The woman was a contradiction. Ice and fire. She'd kissed him back with far greater intensity than he'd expected, proving she was attracted to him. There had to be more behind her request to wait, and he was determined to understand it, but for now, he needed to go back downstairs where he could keep an eye on her, while keeping his hands off her. It was a challenging proposition.

The storm was picking up in intensity. She wondered if she should return to the storm shelter. Where had Zach gone?

Her emotions were raging. Everything she'd believed about this marriage was turned on its side with one intense kiss. Her thoughts of a passionless marriage dissipated as he kissed her with an intensity she hadn't known possible.

He'd asked her how she felt, but she didn't have a straight answer since anything she said would reveal more than she was ready to share. She wondered if she was being unfair to him by not voicing her thoughts and feelings. Then she remembered Nikki and decided she wasn't. He hadn't divulged everything, why should she?

Water crept in under the foyer door and she felt panic bubble up. A loud bang caused her to jump, as something hit the house. She cowered in a corner. A moment later, Zach reappeared. "Addison, where are you?"

"I'm here."

He hurried over and stood in front of her, his gaze filled with compassion. "I'm sorry. I shouldn't have left you."

She didn't speak but took the hand he offered.

"Come with me. We'll go back to the shelter."

He opened the shelter, and she descended the stairs ahead of him. When he joined her, he guided her to a seat by the far wall.

"It was a palm tree. The noise," he said.

"Oh?"

"It broke through the roof in my mother's room. We'll have a full-blown flood now that the water has free entry."

"I'm sorry."

"It's fine. Nothing that money can't fix."

"Are we safe here?"

"I won't let anything happen to you. Just stay inside with me."

"Why?"

"I'd think that was obvious."

"No. I mean, why did you kiss me and then run off like that? Did I do something wrong?"

"No. Your response to my kiss told me everything I needed to know. It was just right."

"Then why did you leave?"

"My adrenaline was crazy high from fear of losing you to the storm. I left because you told me you aren't ready for more than kisses. I'm sorry if I hurt you, but I'm giving you the time and space you requested."

She lowered her eyes to the ground.

He lifted her chin gently. "All you have to do is say the word. Tell me when you're ready for more. I'll be pleased to oblige."

"I'm sorry I panicked when you left. I appreciate your willingness to wait."

He shook his head and chuckled. "I don't understand you."

"Few people do."

"Have you been frustrating boyfriends your whole life?"

"You have no idea."

He laughed and tucked her close to his side. "For the next few hours, while we wait for the storm to pass, let's pretend we're kids. We'll forget about the rings on our fingers and go back to being buddies until we're safely in Los Angeles."

She let out a shaky laugh. "I think I'd like that." They both wanted more, but his willingness to acquiesce to her desire to wait meant the world to her. The knots in her stomach tightened as she thought about another night together in the tiny space, and what would ultimately happen when they arrived in California. She couldn't push him away forever. Eventually, he would insist on consummating their marriage. The idea of disappointing him and having him change his mind, or worse, laugh at her, made her physically ill.

Zach watched Addison sleep. The storm would be over by now, and they would need to assess the damage the island took. It would break his heart if his tree house was destroyed, but it could be replaced, so he tried not to dwell on it. He admired the curve from Addison's neck to her shoulder. It was her only exposed skin, and he longed to kiss her bare neck, but he knew it would wake her, and she'd likely panic thinking he was pressuring her. It was hard to understand what was keeping them apart, but he planned to show patience and hope that whatever was keeping her from taking that next step would work itself out shortly.

When she finally opened her eyes, he smiled. He could get lost in the depths of her dark eyes. She was a beauty. "Good morning, love."

"Is the storm over?"

"I believe it is." He reached over and ran his index finger along the bare skin from her neck to her shoulder. "I'm going to check out the storm damage."

She shivered at his touch. "I'll come with you."

"I'd like that." He grinned.

A moment later, she was sitting up and adjusting her clothing, so she was better covered. He let them out of the storm shelter, and she followed him to the garage.

"Most of my equipment was destroyed, but I'll try to get something running, so we can take a ride around the island." He stood with his hands in his pockets and surveyed the damage.

"I'll see how much damage the house sustained while you work on that." Her brows drew together as she frowned.

"Sounds good. I'll come find you when I see what I can get running."

Zach found a dirt bike that wasn't water damaged in a raised shed. It needed some work, which was probably why it wasn't in the garage, but after forty-five minutes of tinkering, he had it running. He went in search of Addison and found her raking out one of the gardens. "Do you want to take a ride with me, darling?"

Addison narrowed her eyes in opposition to the endearment. "Enough with that."

"You will learn to love my nicknames for you."

"Unlikely, but I will join you. Let me put this rake away first."

"Leave it. We'll get back to this later."

He swiped at a smudge of dirt on her chin. "I'd like to see if the tree house is still standing."

When they arrived at the dirt bike, she looked at it skeptically. "I'm supposed to ride on this thing?"

"It'll be fun. Hang onto me."

After he mounted the bike, she got on behind him and wrapped her delicate arms around his waist evoking feelings he was trying to bury. It was all he could do to start that bike instead of scooping her into his arms.

When they arrived at the base of the tree that allowed access to the tree house, Addison stared upward. Pulling on the ladder, Zach turned back to her. "Wait here."

She put her hands in her back pockets and rocked back and forth on her heels. "Why?"

"I don't yet know if it's safe, and I don't want you up there if it isn't."

"Did it ever occur to you that I don't want you putting yourself in danger either?" She glared at him.

"You're cute when you're being bossy." He released the ladder and kissed her on top of her head. "I'll be back in a jiffy."

Before she knew what was happening, he'd scampered up the ladder away from her. Following him crossed her mind, but she decided against it. She paced back and forth awaiting his return. Debris from the trees and other rain forest plants covered most of the ground. A beautiful red and white flower lay loose near the base of the tree. She picked it up and sniffed it. It had a sweet fragrance that reminded her of her grandmother's perfume. The usual noisy forest went silent when they arrived on the dirt bike, but the birds were calling again now that the bike was quiet. She reveled in the peace of nature and marveled at how easily the animals seemed to go back to normal after a devastating storm while people felt the effects for months or even years.

Another five minutes passed before Zach reappeared on the rope ladder. When he joined her on the ground, he shook his head. "I think it remains structurally sound, but it sustained wind damage. I'll have to get a crew out here to inspect it and make the necessary repairs.

"Can I go up?"

"It's probably better if you don't until I know for sure that it's safe."

"Then maybe you shouldn't have been up there either."

"You're correct, but it's too late to argue about it. Want to check the boat launch and see if we lost any boats?"

She shrugged.

"I'll take that as a yes." He hopped onto the dirt bike, and she got on behind him.

All was well at the boat launch when Zach found his toys safely tied where he'd left them. He grinned like a schoolboy and once again she questioned her own hesitation. She could enjoy her marriage to this guy she was crazy about, but instead she was hurting them both. There had to be a way to get past her fears. Maybe more time in prayer was the answer. Life had been so hectic, she'd been shutting out God, except when her zealous husband reminded her of His presence. How could she even question his devotion to her, when he was clearly devoted to God? He had his priorities in order, now if only she could get hers back into proper alignment, all might be right with her world, too.

Zach got back on the bike and drove her back to the main house.

He walked up the front walkway, and she followed behind. "This house is sturdy. There is water damage, but it should be safe for us to stay upstairs tonight now that the storm is over. It'll be a few days before mold becomes an issue."

"It'll be nice to sleep in a real bed."

"Didn't enjoy sleeping with your husband on the air-mattress?"

Her face warmed at the comment. "On the contrary, I might've enjoyed it too much."

"I'm glad. Although, when you're married, I'm not sure that's possible."

"It is when we're taking our time to getting reacquainted."

"Ah. Yes. I suppose so." He grinned. "I'm working on developing an increased level of patience. God enjoys teaching me stuff."

She laughed. "My hesitancy is a God lesson for you?"

"Isn't everything in life?"

"I guess so." She considered his words. It was true. Everything she'd been through had taught her a necessary lesson, so what was *she* supposed to be learning from this experience?

Zach took a break from making repairs and watched Addison gathering palm fronds along the beach. The light breeze whipped the golden strands of her hair around her face, and she pushed them back behind her ear. Without the benefit of electricity, she'd been unable to straighten her tresses, so they had a lovely natural wave. The only makeup she wore was a light lip gloss. She was a stunning natural beauty. He chided himself for his train of thought, he'd known her his entire life. There was nothing different about her looks, so why was he suddenly seeing her as some great beauty.

He went back to work. An hour or so later, the battery on his screw gun died, and he had no way of charging it until the generator was repaired, so he set down the tool and trotted over to Addison. "I'll carry those back for you."

She placed her load of debris into his arms and he hurried to the back of the house where the dumpster resided. The lid had blown off and there was no telling if he'd ever find it, but he tossed the rubbish inside and went back to help his wife.

He found her sitting on the beach, letting the water lap at her feet. "You will get soaked sitting there."

"Maybe it'll cool me off."

He sat beside her. "Hot, are you?"

"I am."

"Yes. You are." He grinned but didn't take his eyes off hers. Reaching out, he ran his fingers down a strand of her hair. "It's as silky as it looks."

"I thought we were buddies until we got to California."

His fingers caressed the bare skin on her back, and she sighed in pleasure. His gaze didn't waver. "Is that what you want, Addison?"

The minuscule shake of her head was all the encouragement he needed. His lips took hers before traveling down her neck. She gave a sharp intake of breath and within seconds they were lying in the sand entangled in each other's arms.

The sound of an engine interrupted the blissful moment. He groaned as she scurried away, and he looked out over the water to see who was disturbing his first chance at a real honeymoon.

A yacht approached, so he waited for them to come closer. A man yelled. "Is everyone okay here?"

"Yes. Generator is out, but we're both fine."

"We saw on the radar that Andros got a direct hit, so we went there to help with rescues. We've been at it all day, but we're heading back to Nassau now. Why don't you two join us? We didn't sustain much damage."

"Will I be able to get a call out from there?"

"Absolutely. If you want, we can radio from my boat and have someone make a call for you."

"That would be fabulous." He looked back toward the house. "Let me get my wife. She ran off when she heard the engine."

"Not the friendly sort?"

"A tad bit shy."

"My wife's down below. I'll have her come up. Maybe seeing another woman will put your wife at ease."

"Thanks. I'll be back in a few minutes."

"I'll get the dinghy out, so I don't ground the boat."

"Much obliged."

Zach went off in search of his bride. He found her in the master bedroom. "Why did you run off?"

"We shouldn't... it was a mistake."

"Addison, we're married. We kissed a little. There is nothing wrong with married people kissing."

"How do you feel about me, Zach?"

"Where is this coming from?"

"Do you care for me?"

"You know I do." He took her hands in his. "Do you think I would've married a woman for whom I didn't feel a deep affection?"

"I'm not sure." She took a deep breath. "Did you love Nikki?"

"I thought I did." He locked his gaze with hers. "I could ask you the same thing, Addy. How do you feel about me?"

She looked away from him. "I care for you."

She wouldn't even look at him when she said she cared for him, but in time she might grow to love him. Hopefully, it wouldn't take another twenty-nine years. "Pack a bag, okay? We're going to Nassau with the couple on that boat. From there, I'll have my people come fetch us."

"Won't they be searching for us here?"

"Not if we radio ahead and let them know where we'll be."

"Okay."

"I thought you'd like a hot shower and safe place to spend the night. Am I wrong? I can send them away."

"No. You're right. A shower sounds heavenly. I'm covered in sand."

"In that case, we'll take advantage of the kindness of these nice people who are out doing rescues."

"We're being rescued?"

"Sort of. We're safe here, but you'll be much more comfortable when we get to Nassau."

"Thanks, Zach."

"For what?"

"I know you're doing this for me. You'd stay here if I weren't with you."

"Possibly."

Chapter 9

Addison washed her hair and enjoyed the scent of the luxurious shampoo. They'd been brought to the fancy resort that their rescuers owned. She didn't think they knew who Zach was, but she wasn't sure they'd care. They seemed to be genuinely decent people.

After towel drying her mane and slipping on a sundress, she made her way to where Zach was seated with Benjamin Rees. His wife, Helena, hadn't arrived in the dining room yet. Both men stood when they noticed her.

"Gentlemen."

"You look stunning, darling."

Her jaw tightened at the 'darling,' but she let it slip. It would be rude to correct him in front of others. "Thank you." He looked fabulous himself. She admired the way his polo shirt pulled taut over the muscles in his chest and back.

"Would you care for a drink?" Mr. Rees asked.

"Just water, thank you."

He nodded to a waiter who filled her water glass.

"It seems the storm spared your resort."

"A little wind damage, but nothing compared to what happened over on Andros."

"Did everyone survive?"

"No. Unfortunately, with the island not expecting a direct hit until the final hours before the storm, the proper preparations weren't made. There have been two reported deaths, but several others remain missing."

"That's tragic." She twisted a strand of hair around her finger.

"Yes. It is."

Mrs. Rees came in and her husband stood and pulled a chair out for her. "I'm so glad you could join us for dinner." She said.

"We appreciate the offer of a place to stay and a hot meal."

"Nonsense. It's the least we can do." She smiled warmly. "What will you do next?"

"My assistant is sending a jet to fetch us tomorrow morning. It'll take us home to California," Zach answered.

"Do you spend much time out this way?" she asked.

"Quite a bit, yes. I own the island you rescued us from."

"Wow. Your own island. Nice."

He uncrossed his legs and leaned forward. "It's beautiful. You should come visit us there once we get the place cleaned up."

"We'd like that," Mr. Rees said.

Zach sat up straight and put an arm around Addison's chair. "I was able to get through to the cruise ship. Your mother and the rest of the passengers are having a wonderful time. Their only concern was that we were safe. Once I assured them we were, they went back to their fun."

"Thank you for checking on them."

"Anything for you, love."

Her stomach somersaulted. Was he trying to annoy her? He didn't love her, but he insisted on calling her those silly names, knowing how much it bothered her. She reminded herself that he'd said he cared for her, and that she'd told him the same. She was pretty sure she loved him, so maybe that was why the term bothered her so much. She only wanted to hear that word if he was sincere. If, perchance, he was, she might revel in the endearment.

They said their goodbyes to Benjamin and Helena Rees on the airstrip before boarding the plane. So much had changed since they'd been on the jet a few days earlier. Zach didn't wait for Addison to sit. Instead, he steered her to a seat near the front of the plane. "We will make a stop and pick up some passengers who couldn't get flights out."

"Okay."

"It was the pilot's idea, but I thought it was a good one. He'd heard about the trouble they were having getting home."

"You won't get any complaints from me."

It surprised him how readily she agreed to the plan. "Thanks for understanding."

"How could I not understand? Naturally, you should help people get home when it's in your power to do so."

He had to stop comparing her to Nikki. He'd known she was nothing like the other woman, wasn't that why he'd chosen to marry her in the first place? "I'm sorry."

"For?"

"All of this. I shouldn't have rushed the wedding. You deserved better."

"Stop it. I'm not a child. I married you of my own free will."

There was no question that she was correct, but sometimes it felt like he'd coerced her. Would she ever let her guard down? He hoped so. He wanted her at his side. A true partner. Taking her hand in his, he ran circles along her wrist with his thumb. If she wanted to take it slow, he would acquiesce, but he refused to allow them to drift further apart. She'd been avoiding any physical contact since he'd kissed her in the sand, but she'd been an enthusiastic participant. He remembered how her arms had snaked around his neck and how she'd pulled him closer like she couldn't get near enough to him. He'd inwardly cursed the approaching yacht for its poor timing.

He slid his arm around her and caressed her bare arm. For once, she didn't break the contact. He sucked in a shaky breath when she snuggled closer. His woman was a study in contrasts.

Addison sucked in a breath as Zach's thumb made circles on her wrist. Every touch was sending shocks of pleasure through her system, and she was powerless to control them. She wiped her sweaty hands on her sundress. It was unreasonable to expect him not to touch her. He couldn't possibly know the reaction his touch was inciting within her. She didn't want him to stop, anyway. When his arm slid around her shoulders and he caressed her bare arm with the tips of his fingers, her toes curled in response.

It would be easier to take things slow if she wasn't so attracted to him. When he'd kissed her on the beach, she'd completely given in. She'd stopped fighting him, but then the boat had arrived and kept her from giving herself to her husband.

It was a blessing and a curse. At least if she'd gone through with it, she would know if he would reject her, but she'd been granted a temporary reprieve. She recognized that she was wasting precious time she could spend in his arms, but her past rejection was traumatic, and she couldn't seem to get past it. Her head told her Zach was trustworthy, but her heart wouldn't let her trust.

Her relationship with Seth had ended five years earlier when she'd told him she'd been saving herself for marriage. He'd laughed her to scorn, and she hadn't heard from him since. It stung when she thought about it. Her head knew that the problem was with him, not her, but her heart ached. If there wasn't something wrong with her, why couldn't she keep a man?

Cuddling closer to Zach, she let herself hope he differed from the other men she'd dated. If he was the same guy she'd spent her childhood with, he was her ideal man. All she had to do was find the courage to let him in. She rested her head on his shoulder and he pulled her closer. She sent up a silent prayer asking for what she believed to be impossible, but she knew even the impossible was possible with God, so she held out a shred of hope.

Addison fiddled with her rings as she followed Amy through the mansion. Zach should've been the one giving her this tour.

"Through here is the indoor swimming pool, the sauna, and the hot tub."

"Wow." She was overwhelmed at the enormity of the place as she looked around. The odor of chlorine brought on a mild headache she knew would only worsen if she didn't escape the smell soon.

"Over there you'll find the movie theater, and across from that is the gym. I can get you a fitness coach if you want one." Amy offered.

"I don't think that will be necessary." She grimaced at the thought of working with an over-zealous trainer. No. That definitely didn't sound like her sort of thing.

"Why is it again that Zach had to run off so quickly?"

"A work emergency. It's nothing too serious."

"What kind of work emergency does a computer guy have?"

"Zach isn't just a computer guy. He runs a multi-billion-dollar international corporation. We received a request from the federal government, and Zach is the only one who can authorize the release of the information they're asking for. He may deny the request until they get a warrant. It's mostly in his discretion. He's one of only three people who has access to the information they want."

"Wow. You make him sound rather important."

"He is. And he guards company secrets tightly. Apparently, he guards personal secrets, too, which is why I didn't know about you until a month ago."

"Does he tell you everything?"

"Not even close, but I think he tells me more than most." Amy laughed. "He doesn't let people in easily, but I'm guessing you'd know that since you're one of the privileged few he trusts."

"Yeah. I suppose so." She followed Amy through a long hallway.

Amy nodded. "Why don't we sit down and have a tall glass of lemonade? We can continue this tour later."

106

"That sounds delightful." Addison gave the other woman a grateful smile.

Amy stopped in the kitchen and gave instructions before showing her outside to a deck overlooking a large outdoor pool. She gestured to a table and chairs. "Let's sit a spell."

"How many pools does one person need?" Addison picked a seat that wasn't in the direct sun, and she leaned back in the chair closing her eyes for a moment. A few minutes later a young woman Amy had called 'Misty' brought their lemonades out along with a tray of sliced fruit. "Thank you, Misty," Addison said, grateful for the sustenance.

"Do you mind if I call you Addy?" Amy asked.

"Not at all." She smiled. "Only Zach calls me Addy, but I don't mind it."

"I'm sure this is overwhelming, Addy, but don't let it get to you. He's the same country boy at heart."

"If you say so." Addison squinted. "He seems more Beverly Hills than Lake Bethel to me. He's changed so much I barely recognize him."

Amy grinned. "He may live in Beverly Hills, but he hasn't been changed by it. Not where it counts." She put her hand on Addison's. "Trust me. He's kind and down to earth, all this is window dressing. It's nothing more than silly trappings to him. He'd be satisfied with a one-bedroom shack."

"Now, that I have a hard time believing."

"It's clear you love Zach, but I'm afraid he's too dense to see it for himself, so you must come right out and tell him how you feel, or he'll clam up, and the two of you will never make this marriage work. I know it's none of my business."

Addison considered the other woman's words. She didn't know they hadn't married for love. "You're correct, it isn't your business, but I sincerely appreciate the advice. I am out of my depth here."

"Please consider me a friend. Zach means the world to me, so I want him to be happy." She made eye contact. "Which means I want you to be happy, as well."

After they snacked on fruit and yogurt, Amy finished the tour ending at the master bedroom. "I'll leave you to it then. Margie should be here first thing tomorrow morning with some dresses for you to try on for tomorrow night's reception."

"Right. A reception. What is it for?"

"Your wedding, silly."

"We had a reception."

"Only a few people were at your reception on the island. This will be for everyone else."

"That sounds overwhelming for our second day back."

"I'm sorry about that. I should've scheduled it for next week. My bad. I got over-excited when I heard you were coming home early."

"It's fine. Thanks."

Zach didn't get home until after ten o'clock. The house was quiet, so he ascended the stairs hoping to find Addison. He found her in the master bedroom. She lay on her stomach in the middle of his bed watching a movie on her laptop.

He set his briefcase down on the long dresser and approached the bed. "What are you watching, darling?"

"Beauty and the Beast." She touched the spacebar to pause it, and sat up to face him.

"The new version or the old one?"

"The old one."

"Is it the same as you remember?"

108

"It is." She picked at her nail polish.

"There's a movie theater in the basement. You might want to give it a try."

"Amy showed me, but a private movie theater all to myself felt a little weird. Maybe I'll try it when you're around."

"I don't know how much of the movie you'll get to see if I'm around."

She shook her head. "All of it."

"I'm not so sure about that." He yawned and stretched his arms overhead.

"Long day, huh?" She rubbed the back of her neck.

"Yes. It was." He walked closer and grasped one of the columns on the mahogany four-poster bed. "How was your day?"

"Awkward. It felt weird being shown around your house by your assistant."

"It's *our* house," He said in a quiet voice. "I'm sorry I wasn't here to show you around."

"Amy explained why you had to be at work." She rubbed her hands on her jeans. "I understand."

"Do you want to come downstairs with me? Or, if you'd rather, I can stay up here with you."

"I'll come downstairs."

"I'm famished." He moved to the doorway.

"Marvin put a plate aside for you." She scampered out of the bed.

"How did you like his cooking?"

"The food was outstanding, but it was weird having him cook for just me."

"He didn't just cook for you. He had to cook for the rest of the staff and for me."

"Yes, but I was the only one at the dining room table." She met him at the door and gave him a peck on the cheek.

"That's my normal."

"I'm sorry about that." Little creases formed between her eyes when she frowned. "That shouldn't be anyone's normal."

"Don't be sorry. My fortune is about to change. I can now share most of my meals with my enchanting wife."

They walked side by side down the hall, and then down the curved staircase, when she turned down the wrong hallway, he gently turned her around by slipping his arm around her waist and steering her the other way. "It's this way to the dining room, love."

"Are you ever going to stop with the pet names?"

"Not until you learn to appreciate them."

"I don't think that's going to happen, but I am getting used to them."

Chapter 10

Addison came out of the walk-in closet, looking stunning in a cream-colored dress fitted in the bodice and flared near the knees. She'd straightened her hair, and it had a lovely shine that begged him to touch it. She did a little twirl when she noticed him staring. "Do you like it?"

"I do." His voice came out huskier than usual. He cleared his throat.

"The dress is Dior, and the shoes are Manolo Blahnik. I'm pretty sure they set you back more than I earn in a year."

"I don't care about the money. You look incredible. Did you have fun today?"

"No. I missed you. They forced me to try on clothes I'll probably never wear, while surrounded by strangers. You should've seen the Versace dress they were pushing me to buy for tonight. Plunging neckline and a slit clean up to the hip."

"You should've gotten it to wear for my eyes only." When she smacked his arm playfully, he feigned injury. "Your day wasn't all bad, was it?"

"It was a tad uncomfortable." She took a deep breath and blew it out slowly. "But I got through it, and you're here now. Besides, I have a closet full of brand-new designer clothes that cost more than most people make in a lifetime. Few girls would complain about that."

"It's understandable that you were uncomfortable. I remember the first time I bought a designer suit, there were three people in the room, and I stood there amid them in nothing but my skivvies. It was most embarrassing. For me, it's a necessary cost of doing business. It's easier to look the part than it is to fight it. There are a few eccentric CEOs that prefer ripped t-shirts to business suits, but I don't think I could pull that off."

She laughed. "I can picture your experience rather clearly after today."

"If you think that's bad, you should've seen my face when I got a look at the price tag. I nearly lost my breakfast. These days I don't even blink. Try not to think about it too much, and you'll get used to it."

"I doubt that."

"I'm sorry about this last-minute reception, Amy didn't mention it until after she'd sent the invites. She likely held out on purpose, so I couldn't tell her no. She's made it impossible for me to refuse." He scowled into the mirror. "Unless I fake a sudden illness. I could do that."

"Please don't." She crossed the room wobbling a tad, as she struggled to stay upright in the sky-high heels she wore. "Amy meant well."

"We had our reception on the island."

"That's what I told her." She fidgeted with her rings. "I'm sure she only wanted to make sure the press got pictures of us. Maybe she thought it would help you lose the playboy image."

"I don't have a playboy image."

"Oh, yes. You do."

"Do not."

"Do so." She grinned. "Stop arguing and I'll help you with your bowtie." She fiddled with his tie. "I like the suit. Armani?"

"No, it's Brioni."

"Well, you look devastatingly handsome in it."

He reached for her waist and held her still. "You think so?"

She nodded, and he bent to taste her lips. "You are incredibly sexy."

Color rose to her cheeks. "Stop that."

"You're adorable when you blush. I should make you do it more often." When he drew her close, her delicate fragrance tickled his senses. "You're sure to be the most beautiful woman in the room. I'm not certain I want to share you." Zach was positive he wanted her all to himself.

He wasn't up to sharing his bride with a room full of men who would devour her with their eyes. Every muscle in his body tightened at the thought, but he forced himself to tamp down his emotions. She was a beautiful woman, but she wasn't anything like Nikki or any of his previous girlfriends. Addy wouldn't go looking for another man's affection. She'd barely warmed up enough to accept his own attentions, but she'd agreed to marry him, so that was something. No. His wife was not the type of woman he would catch in a delicate situation with another man. He clenched his jaw. "I'd rather stay here. Alone. With you."

"You don't have that option."

"What use are billions of dollars when you don't get a say in your own life?"

"Ask your assistant." She slipped her arms around his waist, and his heart took a jolt. This was too good to be true. His lovely wife was initiating further physical contact. "Let's try to enjoy the night, okay?"

"Now that, I can do." His arms tightened around her.

"Don't wrinkle my dress."

"How will I enjoy the night if I don't get you wrinkled?" The words came out in a husky whisper.

"You're incorrigible."

Addison clung to Zach's arm as he casually moved through the crowd of people. She hadn't expected so many celebrities and politicians to be present. Her hands were sweaty, so she constantly dried them on her dress. She'd long ago lost count of how many people had shaken her hand or offered an unsolicited hug. After an hour of mingling her feet were killing her. Her gaze flitted around the room, and she was overwhelmed by the sheer number of people present, many of whom she'd seen on her television screen, but never dreamed of meeting in real life. Glancing down at her designer clothing, she wondered for the umpteenth time that night if she was fitting into Zach's lofty lifestyle.

Amy must've noticed her angst because she approached them and linked arms with her. "Boss, I'm going to steal your wife away for a moment."

"Don't go far."

"I promise not to abscond with your bride."

"Come. Let's go sit down somewhere quiet." Amy ushered her into a courtyard with a fountain. A few people milled about with drinks in hand, mingling among themselves, but they paid them no mind. "You looked like you could use a break."

"Thanks," she said gratefully as she sat on the concrete wall surrounding the fountain and took off her shoes. She rubbed her sore feet. "I don't think I've met so many people in my entire life."

"I felt the same way when I started working for Zach. It's hard to get used to his lifestyle."

"Where are you from, Amy?"

"I'm a Midwestern girl. Iowa."

"California must've been a big change."

"It was, but it's worth it. I enjoy my work."

"You and Zach seem like close friends."

"We are, but he's the boss, so it's an untraditional friendship. I have to be careful how far I push him. Otherwise, he might fire me."

"I guess that's true." Addison giggled. "If he could've fired me this week, I think he would've."

"I can't imagine that being true. I've never seen him so happy."

Addison doubted the truth of the other woman's statement but appreciated her words. "It's been a frustrating week for him. He's probably thinking of how he can send me back home without hurting me."

"I highly doubt it." Amy got serious. "When he told me you were getting married, I initially had my doubts, but then he said you were his best friend, and you'd been planning this wedding for twelve years, I guessed the rest, and he confirmed it."

"So, you know about the marriage pact?"

"I do, and I believe he made the correct decision going through with it."

Addison's face warmed. "You don't think we made a terrible mistake?"

"I'm sure you're thinking you made a huge blunder, but don't let your mind go there. You two belong together. You may think he married you because you were turning twenty-nine and you'd made that agreement as kids, but if you think for one second he would've married you based solely on a teenage pledge, you don't know Zach half as well as I think you do."

"I'm not sure I do know him. I know he doesn't know me anymore."

"That may be true, but he thinks he does, and he loves the girl he remembers. He'll grow to love the woman." Amy smiled warmly. "Are you ready to face the masses again?"

She grimaced "I guess if I must." After putting her shoes back on, she stood. "Thank you for the pep-talk. I needed it. It feels like it's been one step forward and three steps back with me and Zach."

"I'm convinced you two will make it."

Zach mingled with their guests, constantly searching the room for Addison, hoping she would return so he could introduce her to the rest of their guests. He couldn't imagine where Amy had taken her that they'd been gone so long. A professional football player he'd only met briefly on one other occasion cornered him and went into a long rant about the political climate. He wondered why the man had been invited, and then remembered he was a stockholder.

A familiar voice more grating than a fork scraping on teeth broke through the droning of the ballplayer, and his stomach tightened into a hard knot. "Excuse me a moment, please."

Turning to face Nikki, he pressed his lips into a hard line. "What are you doing here?" he asked through gritted teeth.

"Is that anyway to greet me, sugarplum?"

When he turned to scan the crowd for security, she hooked her arm through his. "I only need a moment of your time. Might we talk somewhere more private?"

He followed her through the room hoping to convince her to leave discreetly without making a big scene. She pulled him into a sitting room of sorts with couches and armchairs. It was outside the ladies' restroom, so you had to go through it to get to the restroom. "I don't think I should be in here."

"This will only take a moment, sugar."

She deposited an ultrasound film in his hand. "What's this?"

She flicked the flimsy paper. "This is our baby."

"My baby?"

"Why do you think I kept calling?" She lifted one side of her mouth in a slow smile. "Blocking my number was a new low, even for you."

"What makes you think the child is mine and not Greg's?"

"He can't have kids. He had a vasectomy."

"Or so he told you." He scrubbed his right hand over his face. This couldn't be happening. He wanted children more than anything, a whole house full of them if possible, but not like this. Not with her. Then he thought of Addison. She'd never forgive him. As angry as she'd been about him not mentioning Nikki before the wedding, there was no telling how she would react over a baby. A sinking feeling in his stomach told him exactly what she'd do. She would demand an annulment.

Nikki pushed him down into a chair and climbed on top of his lap. It was at that moment, the sitting-room door banged open, and Amy and Addison walked in.

"Aren't you excited?" Nikki simpered. "We're having a baby!" She undid one of his shirt buttons as she spoke. He pushed her away, but it was too late. Addison was gone.

Addison stared for a second before turning and fleeing the room. Amy followed.

"You can't trust that woman, Addy." Amy had to run to keep up with her. "She's a liar and a cheat."

"He didn't look innocent either. She was sitting in his lap."

"I don't think it was what it looked like."

"How could it not be?"

"At least give him a chance to explain."

She let out a groan. "Fine, but not here. I'm going back to the house. If he wants to talk, send him home."

"Wait. I'll drive you."

"I'll take a cab."

"I don't think that's a good idea."

"Why not?"

"You do not understand how high profile you are now, do you?"

Addison pinched the bridge of her nose, and bit down on her tongue to keep from lashing out at Amy. This wasn't her fault.

"You're Zachary Williams' wife. It's not safe for you to go anywhere alone."

Her hands balled into fists and her fingernails dug into her palms. "I can't live like this."

"It's too late to make that decision. You're already married." Amy tilted her head. "I'll get us a car. I'm coming with you, it's safer that way."

A few minutes later, a limousine took them back to Zach's mansion. Amy followed her to the master bedroom and made herself comfortable on a loveseat, pulling her feet up under her and taking out her phone. She tapped on the device, and Addison was certain she was messaging Zach. It didn't matter.

She threw her belongings into a suitcase she found in the closet. He could keep the designer clothes; all she was taking was what she'd brought into the marriage.

Ten minutes later Zach walked into the room. Amy stood, picked up her heels from the floor beside her, pursed her lips, and shook her head at Zach. "Fix this." She bit out the words.

A few minutes later Addison heard the front door close. They were alone or at least as alone as they ever would be in his enormous mansion filled with staff.

She stopped what she was doing and stared at her husband. Husband. What a joke. He was no more her husband than he was Nikki's. And whose fault was that? How many times had she pushed him away? She blew out a breath she hadn't realized she was holding.

Sinking down onto the loveseat Amy had vacated, Zach whispered, "It wasn't what it looked like."

Her voice raised an octave, as she squeaked out, "Then what was it, Zach? I didn't give you what you wanted soon enough, so you were going to get it elsewhere. That's what it looked like. What exactly did I walk in on?"

"She sat on my lap as the door opened. I pushed her away, but you were gone."

"What about the baby? I heard her say something about a baby."

"I don't know." He shook his head before dropping it into his hands. "She showed me an ultrasound and claimed the child is mine."

"Is it?"

"I can't know that." He lifted his head and stared at his hands.

"Did you keep the ultrasound?"

"She took it with her."

"I'm sure it will be in the gossip columns tomorrow."

He crossed the room and stood a few feet in front of her. "I didn't mean for this to happen." He fell to his knees. "You know how it is. We were planning to get married. I thought she was the one. I don't fool around with every girl I take out despite the playboy image you claim I have."

"No, Zach. I don't know how it is." Her words were barely above a whisper. "I'm not sure I can be the woman who keeps a child's parents apart."

"I didn't know about the baby." He groaned. "Please don't leave me."

She fell to the floor beside him and took his left hand in both of hers. Her finger traced his wedding ring. "What are we going to do?"

"We'll get through this together if you're willing to stay with me." He lowered his forehead, so it rested against hers. "If there is a baby *and* I'm the father, we'll fight for custody."

"You know they don't like to take children from their mothers."

"If I have to, I'll show the court videos showcasing her explosive temper. She's put on a show for the cameras around here many times since we broke up, but I'm hoping it won't come to that. She was cheating on me, so it could be Greg's child."

"I wonder how long you must wait to find out."

"If she'll agree to the test, we can find out now."

"Marry her. I'll give you an annulment, and you'll be free to be a family."

"I might've been an idiot to get involved with her, but I will not marry that vindictive woman. Don't remind me how close I came to doing just that."

"But she may be carrying your child. How far along is she?"

"Three months."

"Did you truly push her away when she climbed onto your lap?"

"I did."

"Too bad there isn't a camera in the sitting room."

"Don't you trust me?"

"Against my better judgment, I trust you." She sighed. "I believe you."

"Will you stay with me, Addy?"

"I will." For now.

He pulled her into a hug and held her so tightly she struggled to breathe. It was in that moment that she recognized how much she cared for him. Leaving him would tear her apart, but if he decided to try to make it work with Nikki and the baby, she would go.

Chapter 11

Zach got to the office before seven. Amy was already at her desk. "Good morning, boss."

He stepped around her desk. "Good morning, Ames. Do you ever sleep?"

"Of course not. Too much to do at Fractal Enterprises." She offered a smile. "Did you fix things with Addison?"

"Yes."

"She's staying?"

"She is."

She took a sip of her coffee. "I'm glad. If you let her get away, you're a fool."

"Don't you think I know that?"

Her look turned harsh, and she glared at him. "What were you thinking going in the ladies' room with Nikki in the first place?"

"It wasn't the ladies' room. It was the room beside it." He crossed his arms over his chest. "She dragged me in there."

She lifted one delicate eyebrow. "You're twice her size. She couldn't have forced you to go anywhere you didn't want to go."

"I didn't want to make a scene."

"Next time, boss, make a scene. It'll be much less disruptive to your personal life."

"Maybe we should get some work done instead of worrying about my love life."

She stood and placed both of her hands on her desk leaning toward him. "I like your wife. I don't want to see her get hurt."

"The last thing in the world I want to do is hurt Addison." He drummed his fingers on her desk.

"Then prove it. Make her feel like she's the only woman in the world."

"How do I do that?"

"You start by going home. Your honeymoon was cut short, and here you are in the office for the third day in a row. Have you taken her around and shown her the area? Does she know where to go shopping or get her hair done?"

"I was hoping you would help her with the girly stuff."

"I will, and I'll have fun doing so, but make an effort. Let her know how much you care about her."

"You think I should go home?"

"I know you should unless you want her to over-think last night and be gone when you get home tonight."

He shook his head. "Good point. I'm gone. Text me if any fires come up that you can't put out on your own."

"There won't be any. Now go. Take care of your bride."

"Ames?"

"Yeah?"

"Thanks. You're a great friend even if you are a pain in the tush."

She pointed to the elevator. "Go!"

Addison sat on a bench in the garden. Her plans for the day were non-existent. What did the wife of a billionaire do? She thought wistfully about her job back in Wilkes-Barre and wondered if there was any possibility of continuing her work for them. She knew the answer without asking the question. If the request came from Zach, she was certain they'd let her keep working, but relying on him was out of the question. There had to be another way.

Maybe she could start one of those YouTube channel video blogs or vlogs as they were called. With such a famous husband, she was bound to get lots of hits. Only, that would be another way of using him to further her career. What could she do that wouldn't involve him? She could go on interviews using her maiden name. That might work, until they discovered she was Zachary Williams' wife.

She picked a flower and held it to her nose. A horticulturist she was not. Identifying flowers was beyond her limited scope. All she knew about the purple flower she held in her hand was that it was lovely. When she heard a car pull up, she smoothed her hair and strolled back into the house. Someone else would answer the door, but she wasn't sure if they would expect her to greet the visitor.

When she heard Zach's voice, she smiled, wondering what he'd forgotten that brought him back to the house so soon. Greeting him in the foyer, she asked, "What brings you home?"

"You."

"Me?"

"I thought we'd spend the day together."

"Really?" Her eyes widened, and she took a step back. "I thought you had a busy day planned at work."

"Amy will delegate everything I had on my agenda. I'm all yours today." She sensed Amy was behind the change of heart, and she was grateful to the other woman.

"I like your assistant. She's something else."

He chuckled. "Bossy. That's what she is."

"So, what did Amy suggest we do today?"

"She thought you might want to see the sights, do some shopping, and that kind of thing. I told her shopping sounded more her speed than mine."

"You might be right there. I'd rather shop with Amy than you."

"I won't take offense." He grinned. "I thought we'd start off the day on a trolley tour, then have lunch, and take a walk through the park."

"You're going to go on a touristy trolley tour?"

"I'll pull my baseball hat down low and wear dark sunglasses. Nobody will know it's me. It'll be fun taking part in a tour. What do you say?"

"I'm game."

Zach enjoyed feeling Addison's leg pressed up against his on the trolley. He set his hand on her knee and wondered if every incidental touch registered for her as acutely as they did for him.

It had been a long while since he'd done anything touristy and it felt good to be out among people. Most of his time was spent sheltered on his grounds or in his offices. Addison rested her hand on top of his, so he laced his fingers through hers. He was rewarded with one of her heart-stopping smiles.

126

He whispered in her ear. "They're about to point out our home, so try to keep a straight face." She snuggled closer. He could definitely get used to her affectionate side. The surrounding sound seemed to fade, and everything melted away from his consciousness until all that was left was her. He felt blessed to have her for his wife. "I made reservations at Spago, but if you'd prefer to eat elsewhere, I can cancel them."

"Can we get chili dogs somewhere?"

"Sure. I'm not sure where they serve chili dogs, but we'll find them. I'll text Amy. She'll know."

"Don't bother Amy. I don't care where we eat, I was only teasing knowing how healthy you Californian beach boys are."

"I'm an Endless Mountain boy. Pennsylvania through and through."

"Sure, you are."

Amy had been correct, Addison had needed this outing, but so had he. He had a feeling that every second spent with his wife would bring a huge return on investment. He tucked his arm around her as they passed their gated home to the 'oohs' and 'ahs' of their fellow passengers. It wasn't often he thought about how fortunate he was to afford such luxury. Most of the time it felt more like a fancy prison but seeing it through their eyes gave him a different perspective.

He whispered in Addy's ear again "Do you know how glad I am to have you beside me?"

"No. Why don't you tell me?"

"Maybe we should get off the trolley here and walk home."

"I think we might get some strange looks."

"I'm not sure how much longer I can wait to get you to myself."

"They promised me a peek at Reese Witherspoon's house and I'm not leaving this trolley until I see it."

He laughed. "I'll be happy to call her and get you a private tour."

"No, thanks. I prefer the tourist experience."

"Whatever makes you happy, love."

It surprised him that she didn't correct him, but maybe today she'd be his without over-thinking it. He'd like that.

They were still laughing when the limo dropped them off at the front door. Addison sensed Zach on the stairs behind her. When she arrived at the master bedroom, he caught up to her and leaned against the door frame. "Did you have a nice time today, love?"

"Yes. Thanks for taking the day off to spend with me." She smiled. "Thank Amy for me, too."

"You can thank her yourself. She's making plans for you two to go to the spa next Saturday."

"That's a plan I can get behind."

"I guess I should head to my room down the hall."

"How long do you think we have before the staff start asking questions?"

"They'll never ask us directly, but I'm sure they're already talking about us amongst themselves wondering if there is trouble in paradise." His expression grew serious. "Is there? Are we going to be okay, Addy?"

"I'm sick about this Nikki thing, but I'll be by your side throughout it."

"Will I ever be welcome in our bedroom?"

"Let's take it one step at a time, okay, darling."

He grinned. "You can call me whatever pet name you like. It won't get under my skin like it does yours."

"Are you sure about that, lovey dovey?"

"Maybe not that one." His eyes bore into hers until shivers ran up her arms. When his gaze dropped to her lips, she could barely breathe, but she wasn't about to move away and mess up the chance for another superb kiss. She bit her bottom lip in anticipation, but then his lips lowered to meet hers and she was lost in the moment. He stepped inside the room and closed the door behind them before backing her up against the interior of the door and continuing their kiss. She breathed in the spicy scent of his aftershave and ran the tips of her fingers along his five o'clock shadow. Her arms draped around his neck, and she tangled her fingers in his hair. She wasn't sure she could handle the physical feelings he was evoking in her, let alone the emotional toll falling in love with him would take on her heart. All it would take was for him to change his mind, decide he no longer wanted her, and her world would shatter.

A buzzing noise pulled her out of the moment. "It's your cell, Zach."

"What?" he asked breathlessly.

"That vibrating noise is your cell phone."

"Oh, that."

He turned it off and slid it back into his pocket.

"Aren't you going to see who it is?"

"It can wait." A slow smile spread across his face. "Now, where were we?"

She ducked under his arm and walked across the room to the window. "We were getting a little too passionate for a couple who is taking things slow while we wait to find out if you're going to be a daddy."

His eyes flashed. "That's not why we're waiting, so don't pretend it is." He glanced back at her with a hard look before leaving the room and closing the door gently behind him.

He was keeping his emotions tightly controlled, but she wasn't sure how many more times she could send him away before he would decide she wasn't worth the trouble. He'd been patient with her, but his patience had limits, and she feared he was nearing them. Tears burned behind her eyelids, but she fought to keep them from falling.

Zach appeared in the doorway of their bedroom. "Church starts at 10:30."

She slid out of bed, donned her bathrobe, and walked over to him. "I think I owe you an apology."

"Save it."

When she reached up to touch his face, he pulled away from her. "I'm sorry. I shouldn't have said what I did last night. You were right. It had nothing to do with the baby."

His blue eyes were as hard as steel. "I'm going to get one of my suits from my closet." He brushed past her and entered his walk-in closet.

She followed. "Are you punishing me?"

He whirled on her. "No, Addison, that's your department." After grabbing the first suit in the row, he draped it over his arm and left her in the closet. She followed. When he reached the door, he turned back to face her. "If you're joining me for church meet me downstairs at 10:00."

"Aren't we going to have breakfast together?"

"I'm not very good company right now. I'll have Marvin bring something up for you."

Addison flopped down on the loveseat and stared at the door Zach had exited. She hadn't realized how mad he'd been. Why did she keep making such a mess of her marriage?

True to his word, Zach sent a tray up for her filled with her favorite breakfast foods. She barely touched it but appreciated that he'd tried to be kind even in his anger. Tears filled her eyes, but she forced herself to get ready for church. Sitting beside him throughout service would be painful if he wasn't willing to forgive her. She took a conservative dress from the closet and laid it across the bed. Then hurried to shower so she could be ready in time.

Zach was waiting by the front door when she got downstairs.

"Ready?" he asked.

"I am."

"Where's your Bible?"

"In Pennsylvania."

He raised a single eyebrow.

"Oh, you mean the one you lent me. I'll run up and get it." She moved as fast as she could and returned to his side a few minutes later.

He held the door open for her. "After you."

A sleek Aston Martin was waiting for them. After opening the passenger door for her, he waited for her to get in, and then hurried around to the driver's side.

"I wasn't sure you remembered how to drive a car." She teased, hoping to lighten the mood.

"This baby is much more than a car." He let out a frustrated breath. "I'm sorry, I know I was rude this morning. You know I can't sit in church beside you if I don't forgive you, so let's move past this. Okay?"

"I don't blame you. I was wrong."

"Yeah. Well, I'm not blameless. You deserve a husband who's more self-reflective and less quick to condemn."

She reached for his hand but added nothing to the conversation. It wasn't her job to argue against whatever was going on his heart and mind. If he was willing to forgive her, that was enough for her. Maybe soon, she'd be able to forgive herself for causing such division in her own marriage.

Sitting beside his lovely bride, he grimaced as the pastor began with a passage about God's design for marriage. Most of the sermon focused on the church as the bride of Christ, but there were enough references to marriage between a man and a woman to sufficiently put him in his place. He hadn't expected wedding Addison to be a problem. Marrying someone he knew well, and in whom he trusted should've proved an easy, comfortable union, but something had gone wrong. Maybe what she said was true, and they'd both changed far more than he'd realized. Regardless, they'd said their vows, so now they'd make it work somehow. Since he'd picked her up in rural Pennsylvania, everything had been about him. He couldn't think of much he'd been forced to change to fit her into his life, but her whole life had been turned upside down. How was it that he somehow resented her for the one area she held back? There was only one thing she wasn't ready to give, and if he cared about her, he'd be patient. It had only been eight days and waiting that long was hardly unreasonable.

He reached over and took her hand in his. She smiled hesitantly up at him, and his stomach knotted at the realization that her hesitation was his fault. If he'd been kinder to her when she'd apologized that morning, she'd likely be more confident. When the pastor finished the sermon, they sang "Just as I Am" for the altar call, and he listened to Addison sing. Shuffling outside with the rest of the congregation, he whispered to her, "Want to go out to eat?"

"Don't you think your car is too expensive to leave outside while we eat?"

"Nah. It'll be fine." He placed his hand on the small of her back and made introductions to the pastor and his wife as they made their way from the church. It was awkward introducing Addison as his wife when his pastor knew he'd been engaged to Nikki so recently, but it was time for him to put the past firmly behind him and move on with Addison at his side.

A special meal with his wife was a good place to start repairing the damage he'd caused to their marriage. He sent a quick text to his pilot and another to Amy. She wouldn't be thrilled at the interruption on a Sunday, but he knew she'd make one call and delegate the task to someone else who would take care of the details. When they arrived at the airstrip, the plane was waiting.

Addison glanced around. "What are we doing here? I thought we were going to lunch." She blinked.

"It'll be dinner by the time we arrive, but they'll serve snacks on the plane, so you don't pass out on me." He grinned. "I want to take you somewhere special."

"I didn't pack a bag."

"You won't need one. We'll come home afterward, unless you'd rather stay the night. In which case, I'll buy whatever you need."

"How can I know what I want if you won't tell me where I'm going?"

"You'll see." He followed her up the stairs and onto the jet.

A little over five hours later they landed in New York City where they were met by a private car that would take them to Trump Tower. Her face was alighted with excitement when he led her into the restaurant. "I hope you like French food."

"I cannot believe we're eating at Jean Georges."

"Why not?"

"It's unreal."

"I assure you it is quite real." The maître d' said before leading them to their table and pulling out Addison's chair.

Zach sat across the table from her. "I hope it lives up to your expectations."

Addison leaned over the table. "The maître d' didn't even ask your name."

"It's a hazard of owning Fractal, I'm afraid. My face has become somewhat recognizable." After taking a sip of his water, he asked, "Did you decide if you want to stay the night or go home?"

"We should go home. Staying overnight might be too much excitement for one day."

"Whatever you wish, darling."

"You will bring me back to New York though, right? I was here once before, but it was for a work conference, so I didn't get to see the sights."

"Absolutely." He loved the way her eyes twinkled, and her face shone with exhilaration. If he'd realized how easily he could please her, he'd have taken her somewhere special sooner. He wasn't a big fan of New York City, but if it brought her pleasure, he'd bring her back often.

The following morning after a few hours of restless sleep, Zach went to work. The excitement of the day before fresh in his mind. He was positive that Addison had a nice time in New York, in fact, so much so that she'd remained unguarded the entire flight home. It was heaven having her cuddle up beside him on the seat. Yet, somehow, by the time they entered his Beverly Hills mansion, she'd frozen up again. It was impossible for him sort out in his brain. He'd thought they'd had a fabulous day, but he must've said or done something to push her away again.

He dropped his head into his hands and rested his elbows on his desk. He'd married her because she was the proverbial girl next door. There was a level of trust he shared with her he hadn't had with any other woman. It seemed like every girl he dated had to stack up to the checklist in his mind, and that list was based on Addison Scott. It wasn't as if he'd picked some random girl to marry.

Only she wasn't Addison Scott now. She was Addison Williams. He'd made her his wife, but he'd rushed her into it. No. He wasn't being fair to himself. He'd asked her abruptly, and he hadn't taken the time to court her properly, but she'd agreed and had charged into marriage alongside him. Did she love him? He'd asked her how she felt about him after the wedding. He didn't doubt she cared for him as a friend, but he wondered if her feelings had grown as his had. Was he her everything as she was his?

How was he supposed to get work done with his wife haunting his thoughts?

Absentmindedly, he picked up the office phone when it rang. "How did you get my direct number?"

Amy had blocked Nikki's known numbers, but all she'd had to do was call from another phone. The filth she was spewing tempted him to hang up, but when she said she would get to him through Addison, he swallowed hard. "If you dare touch her, you'll regret it." He knew his threat was meaningless to the woman on the other end of the line. When all that was left was a dial tone, he placed the phone carefully back on the receiver.

If he could get Addison to come to work with him, maybe he could protect her from Nikki. He wasn't sure her threats held any real weight but didn't want to take any chances. Besides, he might be able to concentrate on his work knowing his wife was close by. The time they spent together at work might help them reestablish their friendship, and that was definitely worth a try.

He picked up his phone. "Ames, come in here, please."

A minute later the petite brunette appeared in his doorway. "What do you need, boss?"

"Find my wife a job here."

"Doing what?"

"She designs and codes websites. Bring her here."

"I'm not sure she'll agree to your plan."

"If she won't, put her on the phone with me. I'll talk her into it."

"That isn't the kind of conversation you have on the phone, Zachary."

"Fine. Then bring her in here, and I'll talk to her." He shoved the keyboard out of his way. "I need her here."

"I'll try."

An hour later, his wife was standing by the window in his small conference room, dressed professionally in a skirt that came just below her knees, with a silk top, and a matching jacket. He couldn't take his eyes off of her in that outfit. It took several deep breaths to keep himself from pulling her into his arms. "You look like a schoolteacher."

"Is that a good thing?"

"Definitely."

"What am I doing here, Zach?" She studied him.

"Didn't Amy tell you?"

"She told me that you needed to talk to me about a job."

He put his hands in his pockets. "Right. You said you wanted to work and keep doing what you did before we got married."

"I know what I said."

"What happened there? Are they going to let you work remotely?"

"No. They can't make an exception for one person."

"Good."

"What do you mean 'good'?" She scowled. "It is not good."

"That came out wrong. I only meant that I want you to work here, but if you were working for them, you couldn't work here."

"I can't work for you."

He flopped down into the chair at the head of the conference table. "You're my wife. This is my company. You can and *should* work here."

"This is the share-holders company now that you've gone public."

"I'm still the CEO."

"Working together is a bad idea. You'll get sick of having me around. Besides, I have no idea what you do here."

"Amy will help you find your niche within the company. Please. I need you here at the office with me."

"What are you afraid of Zach?" She crossed the room and sat beside him, leaning forward and taking his hands in hers.

"I'm not Nikki. I won't be out fooling around with another man while you're at work."

"I would never think that of you."

"Then what is it?"

"I want you here."

"Yes. We've established that, but why?"

"I'm not sure. Can't you accept that I don't want us to be apart?"

"We've been apart for twelve years."

"I know. We never should've let that happen."

He couldn't blame her for being skeptical about working together. "Please work here. Give it a chance. Try it for a week. If you hate it, I won't ask you to come back."

"Okay. I'll try it for you, but I don't think it'll work." She stood.

He rose to his feet and took a step toward her. She held up a hand to halt him. "It definitely won't work if you start that." He swallowed hard but tamped down his emotions. She'd agreed to give the working arrangement a try, so at least he wouldn't have to worry about her being in any kind of danger. Besides, if she spent too much time at home alone, she might start thinking, and talk herself into leaving him.

Chapter 12

Introductions were made as Addison followed Amy through the office. She knew she wouldn't remember a single name by the end of the day, but she tried to make eye contact, smile, and shake hands with every person she encountered. It was exhausting.

When she was brought to a room with a dozen computer screens, Amy pointed to a chair. "This is where the magic happens. The boss man makes the final decisions, but we have two teams who bring him ideas. One team focuses on form while the other team concentrates on function. This is my best guess at where you'll fit into the picture. I'm hoping you can fit the two pieces of the puzzle together, filter out any extra noise, and only present Zach with ideas worth further exploration. That would cut down on his duties substantially thus freeing him to be home for dinner." She strode to the door before turning to face Addison again. "Does that sound like something you'd be interested in doing?"

She nodded in response. "It's overwhelming at the moment, but once I get to know everyone and see what they're working on, that should be something I can do well."

"Excellent. Zach needs to work on priority projects. Lately, he's been juggling too much, and it keeps him running in circles. If you could take some of that responsibility from him, it would be a blessing for all of us."

"May I ask you something?" At Amy's nod, she continued. "Do you think he only wants me here, so I'm not sitting home moping about losing my former job?"

"No." Amy smiled. "He can't even tell me why he wants you here, but it isn't that. I think he's got it in his head that he'll think about you less if you're in the building. Honestly, I'm certain he's got that wrong, and it'll be far worse with you here, at least in the short-term, but, hopefully, in time he'll get past this newlywed syndrome."

"Is he keeping tabs on me because he's afraid I'll cheat on him?"

"Maybe." She nodded. "It's possible. He's been burned more than once."

"I would never cheat on Zach."

"Good. He's like a brother to me. I don't want to see him hurt again. That last girl was a piece of work. Harlot is too good a word for her."

"I'm sure I agree, but if she's carrying his child. I want to try to be more generous."

"You're a bigger person than I am. I want to stab her in the eye with a fork."

"Don't hold back. Tell me how you really feel."

"Sorry." She scrunched up her face. "Too much?"

"I'm glad you're in his corner."

"Zach's not an easy man to work for. He's demanding, he can be a bit scattered, and he expects everyone who works here to give one hundred percent to work during office hours, but he's also kind and treats everyone as an equal. I've never heard him talk down to anyone. The generous pay and substantial time off don't hurt either."

"I'm glad I didn't run home the other night."

"Not as glad as Zach is."

"I'm worried. We keep hurting each other, and I'm afraid I don't know how to be a proper wife."

"Don't rush it. He doesn't yet know how to be a husband either. You two have your whole lives ahead of you. You can learn about marriage together, the same way you learned about life when you were kids and take the lessons as they come."

"That's it!" She smiled.

"What's it?"

"I think you gave me the answer I've been searching for. I have to find Zach."

Amy pointed. "Just down that hall and to your left. His name is on the door."

She knocked on Zach's office door feeling silly.

He hollered, "Come in."

After entering, she closed the door behind her and leaned against it resting her eyes for a moment. "Amy said something that brought everything into perspective."

"What's that?"

"We can learn together. The same way we learned lessons as kids."

"Learn what?"

"How to be married. We don't have to know it everything now. We can trust each other and learn how to be husband and wife together. All we have to do is be together and trust that the rest will come."

His gaze traveled from her eyes to her feet and back up again, finally settling on her face. "You're cute when you have an epiphany."

"Whatever." She crossed her arms over her chest.

He rose to his feet and closed the distance between them. "I'm going to kiss you now, Mrs. Williams, and I hope you won't run off."

She unfolded her arms and allowed her hands settle on his hipbones. "I look forward to—" he cut off her words when he lowered his mouth to hers.

It was some time before he raised his head and looked into her eyes. "Thank you for agreeing to work here. I can't think straight without you close."

"You're crazy."

"I need you." He kissed her again, slowly. A knock interrupted the moment. "What?" he growled.

The receptionist hesitated for a moment before announcing the call without first opening the door. "I'm sorry, sir. Your phone seems to be on mute. Nikki West is on line three."

"Tell her I'll call her back."

"You should take the call." Addison edged the door open and squeezed through it. "I'll be in the break room if I can find it."

"I can show you." The willowy redheaded receptionist offered. She knew Amy had introduced her earlier but couldn't remember her name.

She followed the other woman down the hall. Her stomach churned as she thought about Nikki's call. Was it about the baby? She wondered if the other woman was pleading for Zach to take her back. It wouldn't be easy, but she'd walk away if he wanted to make things work with her. There was a child involved, so she couldn't stand in their way. He said it wasn't what he wanted, but how could he be so positive when he didn't even know for certain if the baby was his yet. She strongly suspected that it was.

When they arrived in the break room, the woman strolled over to a fancy coffee machine and messed with the buttons. A minute later she handed her a cup of coffee. "I hope you'll enjoy this. It's my favorite. This machine makes so many things."

She brought the cup to her lips. It was sweet, but tasty. "Thank you. This is delicious. I'm sorry, I forget your name. Amy introduced me to so many people today."

"Stacy."

"I'm glad to meet you again, Stacy. Thanks for the coffee. Maybe you can show me how to work this machine later."

The girl beamed. "I'd be happy to." Stacy hurried from the room leaving Addison by herself. Finding a seat, she waited, hoping Zach would think to come find her and tell her how his conversation with his ex-fiancée went.

It was nearly time to wrap-up for the night, and he hadn't been able to find Addison. Hitting his intercom button, he buzzed Amy. "Where is my wife?"

"In her office."

"She has an office?"

Amy hung up and strolled into his office. "What did you want me to do with her? Of course, I gave her an office. She's the boss' wife. Did you want me to sit her in a cubicle somewhere?"

"No. You're right. She should have an office." He scrubbed both hands over his face. "I'm frustrated because I haven't been able to find her. I searched the building for thirty minutes."

"You should've asked me sooner."

"You weren't at your desk."

She pulled her cell from her jacket pocket. "I was in a meeting with your lawyer, but I always have my cell with me."

"Sorry. I know I'm making you crazy."

"What's going on, boss?"

He ran a hand over his face. "Nikki called while Addison was in my office."

"Ah."

"I was rude to that new redheaded girl, Stacy. Apologize for me."

"I will, but do so yourself when you have a chance. She's a superb receptionist. We don't want to lose her."

"Sorry."

"Really, Zach, this is so unlike you. What's going on? I've never seen you be rude to anyone."

"It's Nikki. That was the third time she called today. She's trying to destroy my marriage. She threatened Addison. That's the main reason I wanted her here."

"Maybe we should hire a bodyguard for her."

"I don't know. She'll get freaked out, and I'm sure Nikki is all talk. Don't you think?"

She leaned against the door frame. "I don't know, Zach. You're on your own when it comes to analyzing Nutty Nikki's true intentions. I'm not touching that one. I think I'll stay out of it."

"There's a first time for everything, Ames."

Through the glass wall of her office, Addison watched her husband approach. She enjoyed the open feel of the space, but it would afford little privacy.

Zach leaned his muscular frame against the doorjamb. "You about ready to go home?"

"Leaving already? She glanced at her watch. It's only six."

"I thought we might go home together and have a nice quiet dinner."

"I'd like that." She signed off her computer, grabbed her purse off the chair, and tucked her hand in the crook of his arm.

"Nice office."

"We won't be able to kiss in my office. Everyone will see."

"I'm not sure that would stop me."

"Save the passionate kisses for home." She placed a chaste kiss on his cheek.

"If you insist, but if we're in the privacy of our home, don't feign surprise when the kissing gets out of hand and leads to more."

Her cheeks warmed at the suggestion. "Please be patient with me, Zach."

"I'm trying."

"What did Nikki want?"

"Do we have to talk about that?"

She took a step back and turned to face him. "Eventually, yes, but not right now if you don't want to."

"Thank you." He grimaced. "I want to put her out of my mind and focus on you."

His hand moved to the small of her back as he guided her through the maze of hallways until they arrived at the front doors. "I called ahead for the car to be brought around."

"All this extravagance will take some time for me to get used to. Maybe we can drive ourselves sometimes."

"I know it's a huge change. It was for me, too." He smiled. "We can drive, but I don't have any vehicles you won't consider over-the-top."

"You can buy me a Ford Focus."

"Do they still make them?"

"I don't know, but you can get me a used one if they don't."

"Maybe we can compromise, and I'll buy you a new BMW."

The driver came around and opened her door. Addison slid inside. She heard tires squealing and looked up just in time to see the blur of a blue sports car before it blasted into the limousine.

Zach watched in horror as Nikki's car barreled into the limo his wife had entered and her side of the car was crushed against the brick building. His driver lay on the ground behind the twisted metal wreckage. "Someone call 9-1-1!" He shouted the words as he entered the car through the rear driver's side door and checked Addison's pulse. She was alive, but unconscious. Despite his misgivings about leaving her, he had to check on Javier, so he crawled back out of the car and hurried to where his driver lay still. His pulse was thready, and he was bleeding profusely from his leg. Quickly, he took his jacket and shirt off and tore his shirt, so he could use it to wrap the other man's leg with it.

It felt like time moved in slow motion while he made his way back to Addison. "Darling, wake up." Hot tears ran down his cheeks, and he brushed them away.

Nikki picked that moment to get out of her car. Her face was cut, and she was red from the airbags. "You can't throw me away like so much trash. If I can't have you, she can't either. If you won't leave her, I'll kill her."

Outwardly, he ignored her taunts, but he worried for Addison's safety. What would Nikki do next? "Get her out of here." He shouted to security who'd only just appeared. "This was intentional, and Ms. West is responsible. When the police get here, I want her arrested."

He kneeled down beside Addison, held her hand, and stroked her hair until an EMT insisted he move, so they could transfer her to an ambulance. Once they had the stretcher loaded, he climbed into the ambulance and took her hand in his. "Is she going to be all right?"

"Can't say, but it could be worse. They'll check her out thoroughly at the hospital."

By the time she regained consciousness, he thought he might've worn a hole in the floor from pacing. He crossed to her side and cupped the side of her face in his hand. "You gave me a scare."

"What happened?"

"Car accident. Sort of."

"Sort of?"

"It wasn't exactly an accident. Nikki rammed her car into the limo on purpose. We'll talk about it more later. What do you remember?"

"I remember getting into the car, but it's foggy."

"I will go get the doctor and let her know you're awake."

She closed her eyes. "Try to stay awake for a few minutes, sweetheart."

He hurried to find Addison's doctor. "My wife is awake."

When they returned to the room, Addison's eyes were shut. The doctor hurried to her side with a penlight in hand. "Open your eyes, Mrs. Williams. I have to check your pupils."

She did as directed. The doctor ordered some scans, and once they were read, they released her, but told him to keep a close eye on her since she had a concussion.

Amy picked them up in her personal car. "Nice scrubs. What happened to your shirt, boss?"

"My shirt was a tourniquet for Javier until EMS got there. His bleeding was severe." He grimaced.

"Is Javier okay?"

"He will be, but he lost a lot of blood. They had to do a transfusion."

"I can't believe that nut job went after Addison like that."

"Thanks for the ride, Ames. We don't have a driver on duty now that Javier's laid up, and Addison needs to get home and rest." He shook his head. "That sounded cold. I didn't mean to make it sound like Javier's injuries are an inconvenience. I would've called an Uber, but you know the danger that could present."

"I do." Amy glanced over at him. "Don't sweat it. I know you care about Javier, but we'll have to call in another driver."

"We can talk about it tomorrow." In the morning he'd hire her the best bodyguard in the business. Keeping his wife safe was his top priority.

Addy didn't speak on the ride. He wasn't sure if it was the concussion or the pain medication keeping her sedated. When they arrived home, he didn't invite Amy in because he didn't want to talk anymore about what happened. After assisting Addison up the stairs and into their bedroom, he brought her a nightgown and left the room to give her privacy. When he returned, she was dressed for bed.

"How are you feeling?"

"Like I have three broken ribs from being hit by a speeding car."

"I'm so sorry, love. I didn't expect this to happen."

"I guess your conversation with Nikki didn't go well."

"You could say that." His hands tightened into fists. "She made threats. I should've taken them more seriously."

"How could she put her child at risk like that? To slam her car into ours?"

"I told you she wasn't in her right mind."

"Men say that kind of thing all the time. It doesn't make it true."

"What are you talking about?"

"They have called me crazy, wacky, insane, and more when they couldn't get what they wanted from me."

"I'm sorry. You are none of those things."

"You say that now, but when you find out how little experience I have, you'll reject me, too. I'll never be good enough for you."

Guilt settled in the pit of his stomach. It was wrong for him to let her open up when her system was compromised, but he couldn't stop himself from asking. "What are you saying, sweetheart?"

"That you won't want me anymore when you find out I'm a virgin. A twenty-nine-year-old virgin. I'm a punchline. A joke. Is it any wonder men mock me about it?"

He couldn't believe what he was hearing. He'd married a woman who'd kept herself pure, and she was ashamed of it. Worse yet, he'd rewarded her goodness by shoving a homicidal pregnant ex-girlfriend in her face. He raked his fingers through his hair. There was no easy way to fix this. How could he reassure her that he thought she was perfect the way she was?

"Addison, honey, saving yourself for marriage is commendable. It is such a precious gift, and I would never reject you for it. Purity is the greatest gift one spouse can give another. I only regret that I can't offer you the same." There was a chance she wouldn't remember having this conversation. He wasn't sure if that was a good or bad thing.

She smiled and closed her eyes. "I don't want to lose you, but I don't have a clue what I'm doing. I can't compete with all those other women. I'll understand if you don't want me." He wondered how many women she thought he'd slept with. It had only been two, which was two more than it should've been, but she talked like it was hundreds.

"You're my universe, darling. Don't talk like that." He kissed her forehead. His heart swelled with love for her. When she'd refused him, she'd been pushing him away because she feared his rejection. How had he missed it? There had to have been signs, but he'd been too caught up in his own pain to see them. He needed to prove to her that he could be trusted with her heart.

Chapter 13

Addison sat up in bed and winced. It all came back to her. The blue blur and the crash. She gingerly set her feet on the carpet and prepared to stand. That's when she noticed Zach watching her from the loveseat on the other side of the room. "You scared me. I didn't realize you were in here."

"I've been here all night."

"Why? I'm okay."

"The doctor told me to keep an eye on you. You had a concussion."

"I doubt he meant for you to stay awake the entire night."

"I fell asleep at one point."

She crossed the room and stood in front of him. "Thank you. You're a prince."

He pulled her down, so she was sitting beside him and kissed her forehead. "Now that you're awake, I will go take a shower and wash off Javier's blood."

"You didn't do that yet? That's gross."

"My primary concern was for the welfare of my wife."

"I'm fine. I'll be ready for work in twenty minutes. We can drive in together if you want."

"You're not going to work today."

"How am I supposed to learn the job if I don't go to work?"

"Doctor's orders. You're home for at least a week, and, even then, you need clearance from your doctor."

"I'm not sure I believe you."

"I have the note."

"That you told her to write?"

"Why would I do that?"

"I don't know, but I'll bet you did. What am I supposed to do with myself all day?"

"Rest and get better. I'm staying home with you."

"What are we going to do, binge Netflix shows?"

"Sure. We can even watch chick flicks or Disney movies if you want. Just don't tell anybody."

"You must be feeling guilty if you're willing to watch those. You know this wasn't your fault, right?"

He grimaced. "It sure feels like it was."

"You can't control your ex-girlfriend's behavior."

"I know." He winced. Who knew what Nikki would try next? "Meet me in the kitchen in thirty minutes. We'll have breakfast, and then we'll decide how to spend our day together."

"I'm holding you to the chick flicks."

"Very well."

Zach didn't spend much time in the theater room since he worked long hours, but it was comfortable, and he hoped Addison would enjoy having a movie theater experience in the comfort of their home. It surprised him when she chose a seat near the back. He'd expected her to sit up front in one of the reclining chairs with the armrests in between. It would've been an effective barrier to cuddling, but instead she'd chosen a couch in the shadows along the back wall, and when he sat on the opposite end of the couch from her, she scooted closer to him, leaning her head on his chest. His arm circled her automatically, and he sent up a silent prayer of gratitude. It seemed his lovely wife was finally thawing toward him.

He'd been surprised she'd chosen "How to Lose a Guy in 10 Days," when there were so many newer options available, but she said it was one of her favorites, so he'd shrugged and put it on for her. As she watched Matthew McConaughey on the big screen, he studied her. Memorizing every smile, chuckle, and frown. It was no wonder he'd married her. The woman snuggled up beside him was one-in-a-million, and Zach planned to do everything in his power to keep her at his side.

Nikki was a vindictive monster, but he couldn't deny his own child. It seemed there would not be an easy answer for him. He'd made this mess by not following God's plan of abstinence before marriage. Staring down at his wife, he took stock of his failings and once again thanked the Lord for not allowing more serious harm to come to her the previous night.

Caught up in watching Addison, he didn't notice the movie had ended until she turned in his arms and initiated a kiss. Taking full advantage of her vulnerability, he deepened the kiss and ran his fingers through her silky hair which was full of natural wave. He was glad she hadn't had time to straighten it. It was cuter in its natural state.

Addison grew restless as the week progressed. With Zach at work and her stuck in the house, she wasted too much time on social media. When it finally occurred to her to check out the library, she found a haven in their home. There was an entire section of Christian fiction and another one for Christian non-fiction and research books.

She picked out a few books and retired to the reading nook in the corner of the library. Several hours passed before Misty came looking for her for dinner. "The master is in the dining room requesting your company."

It took every ounce of her self-control to keep from laughing at Zach being referred to as 'master.'

When she arrived in the dining room, he stood and pulled out her chair for her.

"You're always a gentleman." She craned her neck to look up at him.

He gave her a sheepish smile. "I wish that were true, but I have my less than gentlemanly moments."

"I spent time in the library today. It's a fabulous room."

"I knew you'd like it."

"It's terrific."

"Glad you like it. I'm hoping we'll have many a late-night Bible study in there." He bowed his head and asked the blessing.

Her steak was cooked to perfection, and the spinach served with it was delicious. She was getting used to having someone cook for her every night, and when Zach made it home for dinner, it was an extra special treat.

He tilted his head to the side and watched her for a moment. "Good, huh?"

"Magnificent."

"Are you looking forward to your spa trip with Amy tomorrow?"

"I am. A massage will be a real treat."

"You can order one any time. We can even get someone on staff."

"That is unnecessary." She smiled. "I forget sometimes how wealthy you are, the extras are fun, but let's not get carried away."

"The construction crew called about the island."

"And?"

"The tree house is structurally sound. They'll make those repairs immediately, so we should be able to go back there in a month or two." His dimples were pronounced when he smiled. "As for the other house, it'll take longer since they have to rip out the drywall and replace the roof."

"Did they give you a timeline?"

"Six months."

"I'm sure you'll be glad when we can go back to the island." Addison set her fork down.

Zach reached for her hand. "We have a honeymoon to finish."

Her cheeks felt like they were on fire as he gazed at her with fierce intensity. "Yes, we do have to finish our honeymoon." She let herself dream about what it might be like to have an honest to goodness honeymoon. "I'm ready when you are."

"I'll have them expedite the repairs." He grinned. "No expense is too large to keep us off that island."

"We can always go someplace else."

"I think it's only fitting for us to go back to where we said our vows and finish what we started."

Addison was bruised and battered, but this spa day with Amy might prove beneficial. She could certainly use the massage. The Jacuzzi at home had eased some of the soreness, but she wasn't fully recovered.

She'd been looking forward to spending the day with Amy. They'd formed a bond, and she desperately needed a friend.

"You ready to float?" Amy asked.

"The salt thing, right?"

"Yeppers."

"I guess so."

They walked through to a room that led to the private float tanks and then went their separate ways. The experience was so relaxing that she almost fell asleep. Afterward, she showered, dressed, and waited for Amy to finish doing the same. While blow drying her hair, she caught sight of Nikki in the mirror. Terror rose in her throat, but she didn't scream. She stared at the reflection of the other woman.

"So, you think you won, do you?" Nikki snarled.

"I don't know what you're talking about."

"If you think that you, a little country bumpkin from nowhere special, can waltz in and steal my man out from under my nose, you have another thing coming, girl."

"He wasn't your man. He left you when you cheated on him."

Nikki snickered. "Is that what he told you?"

She swallowed the lump in her throat.

"When he found out about the baby, he dumped me. Zach doesn't like kids, but he'll come back when I get you out of the picture."

"How do you propose to do that?" Addison held out her left hand. "We're married."

"You'll march your little self back to whatever back woods place you came from if you know what's good for you."

"Why would I do that?"

"If you don't, it's not only your neck on the line. Zach's next. If I can't have him, nobody can."

"If you love him, you won't hurt him." Even as she said the words, she knew the woman didn't love Zach. It was his money she was after.

"You have no idea what I'm capable of doing. If you don't skedaddle, he dies."

The door opened and Amy appeared. "What are you doing in here? I'm calling the police."

"Don't," Addison said.

"Why not?"

"Just go." Addison glared at Nikki who pierced her with one more hateful look before exiting the room.

"What did she say to you?"

"She threatened Zach's life."

"We need to call the police."

"They arrested her after she rammed our car. She's already out. How long do you think they'll hold her if I call them?"

"I don't know. Probably not long."

"Exactly. Arresting her will not protect Zach."

"Then we should get both of you bodyguards."

"Or I can give her what she wants."

"Which is?"

"I'll go home to Pennsylvania."

"That would kill Zach."

"No. It would save Zach. My leaving can only protect him."

"Addison, you can't leave him. He'll never recover."

"He'll be fine. He married me because of a childhood pact. He can do better anyway. Look at Nikki compared to me. She's model thin with curves in all the right places. Her skin is flawless. I know she's a little wacky, but there are hundreds of women as beautiful as her that would give anything for a chance to date Zach. He won't hurt for attention if I leave."

Amy shook her head. "Don't do this, Addy. Please don't leave him."

"I leave her with you for a few hours while I get caught up on work, and now she's gone." He paced his office. "Where did she go?"

"I think she flew home to Pennsylvania, boss."

"Why would she do that?"

"Nikki made threats against you." She averted her gaze. "I tried to stop her, but she got in a cab, and I couldn't find her."

"Did you call the police? Ask them to track the cab number?"

"I did, but they refused. She's an adult, and she left of her own free will."

He sunk into his office chair and raked his hands through his hair. "I've got to get her back. Call the airlines and see what flights were going to Scranton or Allentown. She could get home easily from either of those airports."

"Should I have the jet readied?"

"Yes. Tell them we're flying to Pennsylvania. We'll give them the specifics once we deduce what flight she might've taken."

"What do you want to do about Nikki?"

"I want to ring her pretty little neck."

"I'm almost certain that will land you in a jail cell."

"What do you think I should do about her? I can't kill her; she may be carrying my child."

"That's just it. The private investigator you asked me to hire says she isn't pregnant. He found a silicone pregnancy belly at her apartment and medical records for an abortion two weeks ago. Before she even told you about the baby."

"How long have you known about this?"

"About ten minutes. I called him on my way here. After Nikki confronted Addison at the spa."

"She murdered my child." He stood and wandered over to the window.

Amy placed a hand on his arm. "We don't know that it was your child."

The pain that sliced through him told him it was. How could she? She'd known how much he wanted to be a father and had manipulated him in the most gut-wrenching way possible.

"Zach?"

He shrugged off her hand and stalked to the door. If he didn't kill her with his bare hands, it would be a miracle, but he'd have to find her first.

"Zach, you need to stop and pray."

Her words stopped him dead in his tracks. He exhaled and tried to regain his composure.

"Let's pray together. Sit." She pointed to one of the chairs on the far side of his desk. He sat with his elbows on his knees and his head in his hands. Amy put her hand on his shoulder and prayed out loud. She asked for guidance and direction, then pleaded for God to help them be merciful to others as He was merciful to them. He didn't want to listen to her words, but knew he needed to hear them. The acid in his stomach churned.

"I'm going to go find her now."

"Nikki?"

"No. Addison."

"Good choice."

The flight home was brutal. Her heart ached more than she'd believed possible. How could she have fallen in love so completely in such a short time? The answer was inescapable. She hadn't fallen in love over the past few weeks, she'd fallen in love with the boy years earlier and only now realized how much she loved the man. He'd changed, but his heart was the same.

She wondered how he would react when he realized she was gone. Would he be relieved or disappointed? Remembering how he sat up all night with her when she got out of the hospital, the truth became clear. He cared for her too, and her leaving would cause him pain.

She told herself she'd made the right decision, and that she couldn't take a risk with Zach's safety, knowing how dangerous Nikki West could be. The woman might follow through on her threats.

Her mother met her at baggage claim at the Philadelphia International Airport. She looked like she might say something, but instead she opened her arms and Addison flew into them.

"I won't ask you why you're home. You can tell me when you're up to it."

"Thanks, Mom."

"We have a long drive ahead of us. Let's get your luggage."

"I don't have any."

"Once again, I'll refrain from asking for now. My car is in short-term parking."

She walked beside her mother to the parking lot. When they reached the car, she got in and felt a wave of grief overtake her, so she closed her eyes and leaned her head against the headrest. Her mother pulled into the airport circle so that she could get on the highway. It was impossible to stop the sobs that racked her body, reminding her of her broken ribs. "Oh darling, I'll get Zachary for upsetting you like this. What on earth did he do?"

"He made me fall in love with him all over again."

"Well, that doesn't sound so bad. He's your husband after all."

Addison inspected her rings through her tears, pulled them off, and shoved them in her jeans pocket.

"Now it can't be so bad that you're seriously contemplating divorce, can it? You don't believe in divorce for anything less than adultery. Did he cheat on you already?"

"No. He didn't cheat on me."

They drove in silence for an hour before her mother spoke again. "I can't stand seeing you in so much pain without even knowing what caused it."

"I'm not ready to talk about it."

"Why don't we stop for some food?"

"I'm not hungry."

"When did you last eat?"

"I don't know."

"Then we're stopping."

"Fine."

Her mother pulled into a rest stop, and they both used the restroom before ordering fast food and making their way to a table. "Eat."

She picked at her french fries and took two bites of her burger. "Good enough?"

"I feel like I'm dealing with a five-year-old child."

"His pregnant ex-girlfriend threatened to hurt him if I didn't leave."

"What?" Her mother reached for her hand and knocked over her soda in the process. "His ex-girlfriend is pregnant? Is it his child?"

"Probably, yes."

"Well, no wonder you left him."

"I'm not leaving him because of the baby. I suggested he go back to her and be a family, but he refused, and once she tried to kill me, she ruined any chance they had for making a relationship work."

"She did what?"

"Zach would've called you, but you were on your way home from the cruise, and once I was okay, I told him not to get you all upset for nothing since I'm fine."

"How did she try to kill you?"

"She purposely rammed her car into ours. Zach's driver was behind the car when she hit it and was seriously injured. I'm okay, a concussion and a few broken ribs, but nothing that won't heal."

"Oh my word, I cannot believe you didn't call me. I would've been there in a heartbeat."

"That there is why I didn't call you."

"So, now this woman has threatened Zachary and you've given in to her demands?"

"What choice did I have? I love him too much to risk his life."

"I understand, but you can't let her win."

"She follows through on her threats. I'm living proof."

"Then call the police."

"They arrested her after she rammed the car, but she's out of jail already."

"There has to be something they can do. Perhaps a restraining order?"

"I hear they do little good."

"It can't hurt."

"Mom, I have to let him go. It's for the best. In time we'll both be fine."

"You won't be fine. Not if you truly love him. Do you think I'm fine after losing your father? Every morning the pain is fresh. I wake up and realize all over again that he's gone. I lean on the Lord, and I get through each day, but it isn't easy. You don't have to mourn for Zachary. Your husband is here and giving him up willingly isn't fair to either of you."

"What do you want me to do? How can I keep him safe?"

"You can't. Trust the Lord for that. He won't take Zach home until He's good and ready. In the meantime, enjoy the time He's given you to be together. And put those rings back on your finger."

She reached in her pocket and pulled out her engagement ring and wedding band and slipped them back on her ring finger. Maybe her mother was right. Why hadn't she prayed about this? Attempting to fix things on her own always failed. If she'd trusted God to begin with, she wouldn't be in this mess. She hoped Zach would forgive her for running off the way she did.

Chapter 14

Zach drummed his fingers on the built-in table beside him on the plane. He noticed Amy's glare and forced himself to stop, but his knee bobbed up and down. The nervous energy needed to go somewhere. Had he lost Addison before he truly had her? Would they play games with each other's hearts for another twenty years? Maybe she was right, and they should put a stop to it now.

No. He couldn't let her go. Now that he had her back in his life, he wanted to keep her there unless she didn't love him. If that was the case, he would release her from her vows. He couldn't let his thoughts go down that path. Another possibility sliced through his mind. What if she hated living in California? Would he be willing to move headquarters? Would he be able to get the board to approve a move? It didn't seem possible for a tech giant like Fractal Enterprises to relocate to rural Pennsylvania, but if it was what she wanted, he'd do everything in his power to make it happen. New York City wasn't too far, he might be able to set up shop there, but the taxes were a killer. He shook his head. Taxes were a secondary concern. His focus was on making his wife happy.

"You're doing it again." Amy's words brought him out of his reverie.

"What?"

"Drumming." She sighed. "Maybe you should join a band and do your drumming on nights and weekends."

"Another one for the bucket list, Ames. Life's too crazy at the moment."

"What did you ever see in that woman?"

"Wasn't that evident?"

"I've never considered you shallow. Would you honestly marry a woman solely based on looks?"

"No. She played her part well. For a while, I believed she was the woman she pretended to be. The longer we dated, the more her vindictiveness showed through, but I was willing to overlook her issues. Heaven knows I have plenty of my own faults. Nikki used my longing for a family of my own against me." He threw his head back and stared at the ceiling of the plane. "No. That isn't fair. I did that. She claimed she wanted kids, so I gave her a ring."

"I'm sorry about the baby, Zach."

His eyes filled with tears. "Until a few weeks ago, I hadn't cried since my junior year of high school when my father abandoned my mother and me. Now, I can't stop."

She handed him a tissue. "Do you think she'll come home?"

"I have to believe she will." He swiped at the corner of his eye.

"You sound confident."

"I'm trying to have faith. Keep praying for us, Ames."

"I will."

166

They arrived at the airport and he hurried inside to the baggage claim area. Her plane should arrive any moment. Since it had a connecting flight, he'd been able to beat it to Scranton. They watched as passengers made their way to the carousel to claim their luggage. Fifteen minutes passed, and the luggage was gone with no sign of Addison. Then a thought occurred to him. She wouldn't have bags. She might've walked right out of the airport and he would've missed her.

He looked at Amy. "We need a car."

"I ordered a car before we left California. It should be here. Let's check."

They exited the building, and there was a car waiting for them. It was a sleek limousine that was about as subtle as a tank. "Maybe the next time we're in rural Pennsylvania we can order a ride that will fit in better. Maybe you could get us a pickup truck," he said.

"Sorry."

They climbed into the back of the monstrosity and headed for Lake Bethel.

When he pulled up in front of Addison's house, all was quiet. He left Amy in the car while he knocked on the door. When no answer came, he walked back to the car. "My mother mentioned a new cabin rental place on Route 487 in Benton, it's only about fifteen minutes from here. Head out there and see if you can book a cabin for each of us. I'll wait here. She'll show up, eventually."

"Are you sure she won't go to her mother's house?"

"She's too independent. If anything, her mother will come here."

"Call me when you know something."

"I won't be able to get cell service without hiking up the mountain, but if Addison comes home, I'll call from the landline."

Addison's mother pulled into the driveway and leaned over the passenger seat pointing toward the stairs. Her eyes followed her mother's finger. There standing on her top step was the man she'd been fretting about the entire ride.

"You should've known he'd follow you."

"He's a fool."

"No. He's in love." Her mother reached over and gave her a hug. "I'm going home, so you two can have some privacy."

Privacy. Something she'd dreaded from the moment she said 'I do.' She let herself out of the car and walked toward her waiting husband.

"Why did you leave me?" His eyes were glassy with unshed tears. "You promised me you'd stay."

"You know why I left. I'm sure Amy told you everything."

"She did, but I deserve to hear it from you."

"Yes. You do."

"You're my wife, you can't run off whenever there's trouble."

"I know."

"What do you mean, you know? If you knew, why did you leave?"

"I didn't know when I left, but I know now."

"Mama Scott?"

"Yeah. She set me straight."

"Can we go inside?"

She took her key out with shaking hands and attempted to insert it into the lock. After her second failed attempt, he gently removed the key from her hand and unlocked the door. He waited for her to enter and then bolted the door behind them. "Let's talk about it, Addison."

She glanced around her house. "I left this place a mess. Clear a spot and take a seat."

"It's not a mess. You're neurotic."

"Did you come all this way to make fun of me?"

"No. I didn't. I came here to bring you home." He glanced around the room. "I need to use your landline." She got him the phone, and he made a call to Amy letting her know that he'd be staying the night. Then, he turned back to her. "How did I miss your plane and get here before you?"

"I flew into Philadelphia. The flight to Scranton was booked to capacity."

"I see."

"I'm glad you came."

"Are you sure about that?"

"I am now."

He gave her his most charming smile as he stepped closer. "Will you come home with me?"

"I'm exhausted. Can we talk about it tomorrow?"

"No. That's a cop-out. Don't you think I'm exhausted? Do you have any idea what I've been through in the last few hours?

"I think I do."

"Then tell me why you left me. I don't want to hear Amy's version. I want to hear yours."

"I don't want to repeat it. It sounds stupid now that I've prayed about it and talked it through with my mother."

"Tell me anyway." He settled in on her couch and waited for her to do the same.

"Nikki threatened to hurt you if I didn't get out of the picture. I believed her, so I left."

"You left to protect me?"

"Yes."

"It's my job to protect you."

"I think we're supposed to protect each other."

"You had to know I would follow."

"I didn't. I thought maybe you wouldn't since I wasn't giving you what you wanted anyway."

"You can't be serious. You'd think that little of me?"

"I don't know. I'm messed up."

"Yes, you are if you think I would let you go without a fight."

"Please don't be angry. I was trying to do the right thing." Her chin quivered, but she couldn't stop it.

"Don't cry. I'm sorry." He scooted closer to her on the couch. "Stop crying. Please. I'm begging you. You're going to make me cry again and twice in one day is too much."

She didn't stop, so he tucked her into his chest and wrapped both arms around her. When she stopped crying, he reached for one of the tissues on the coffee table, and he handed it to her. She moved away from him and dabbed her eyes.

Scooting closer to her, he lifted her chin, so she was forced to look into his eyes. "I have a confession."

She stared at him, waiting for him to continue.

"The night you came home from the hospital, you were a tad loopy and shared some of your secrets with me."

Her face burned as she realized to what he was referring. "Oh, no."

"Darling, you have to start trusting me."

"I trust you."

"No, honey, you don't. If you trusted me, you would've told me the truth without needing to be in a drug-induced stupor."

"I'm so embarrassed." She covered her face with her hands, and he pulled them away from her face.

"Stop hiding from me." He leaned in closer. "I love you."

"You do?"

"Yes."

"I love you, too." Her lips parted, and he kissed her with a tenderness that lent truth to his words.

"Your secret only makes me love you more."

"You're crazy."

"I'm the one who's crazy when you've been hiding something so sweet and perfect? I prayed for a godly wife, but I never imagined I'd be granted one. I don't deserve you."

"Yes, you do." She wrapped her arms around him and put her head on his chest.

A few minutes passed in blissful silence, before she ruined the moment by pulling out of his embrace. "Zach, what are we going to do about Nikki?"

"I'm not sure what the legal recourse is, but I'm sure Amy is on the phone with my lawyer trying to figure it out."

"Amy is a keeper. I don't know where you found an assistant like her, but you should pay her more."

"I know. She's probably the best-paid assistant in California, but if you want me to give her a raise, consider it done."

She smiled.

Zach continued, "I'm sure we should be able to get a restraining order. It's not a perfect solution, but it's a start. After you left, we learned she'd been faking the pregnancy. She was pregnant, but she had an abortion before she even told me about the baby. I had no rights, and she was within her legal right to kill my baby. How messed up is that?"

She put her hand on top of his. "Very."

"The thought sickens me. I made a stupid, foolish choice by being with her, but now I'll live the rest of my life knowing I had a child whose mother murdered him."

Her tone was gentle. "How do you know it was a boy?"

"The ultrasound the private investigator found."

"I'm so sorry." She put her head on his chest and wrapped her arms around him.

"Will you promise me something, Addy?"

She nodded.

"Don't ever leave me again."

"I won't. I'm sorry, Zach."

Bravely, she stood and held her hand out to him.

"I don't want you to take this as a rejection, sweetheart, but let's wait until you're healed. You're hurting from the accident, and I don't want to cause you any more pain."

"Will you hold me until I fall asleep?"

He nodded and took her hand.

Zach was rummaging around in Addison's kitchen when she appeared in the doorway. "Where are we going to church today, darling?"

"I guess we're going to my church in Benton."

"We could go to my mother's church in Shickshinny." He leaned back against the counter and crossed his legs at the ankles.

"That would be fine." She rubbed the back of her neck.

"Nah. We can go to your regular church. It'll give you a chance to tell your friends how the wedding went. It looks like we will have to go out for breakfast after church. There isn't anything in here that's salvageable. I'm surprised you didn't clean out your refrigerator before I picked you up for the wedding."

"I have another confession."

"Do you now?"

"You may want to sit down for this one."

He sat at her kitchen table and watched her as she paced back and forth in front of him.

"I thought you were joking with the emails about getting married. Not for one moment did I think you were serious."

He put his feet up on a chair. "How were you ready? Your mother and sister came to the airport. You had your wedding gown."

She picked at her nail polish while she answered him. "I told my mother about the emails, and she, thankfully, took them more seriously than I did."

"I can't imagine your shock when I showed up on your doorstep. Why didn't you tell me?" He busted up laughing.

She raised her gaze to meet his. Her cheeks were as red as he'd ever seen them. "Embarrassment mostly, and the money you'd shelled out to prepare for the wedding. I didn't want to disappoint you, plus there was that part of me that desperately wanted to marry you and hoped you weren't joking the whole time."

"I think that's my favorite part of you."

"Which part?"

"The part that is madly in love with me even though she hates admitting it to herself."

"It is?"

"Are you glad we're married, darling?"

"More than you can imagine."

He stood and crossed the room taking her into his arms being gentle, so as not to hurt her while her ribs healed. "Do you know how much I love you? How much I've always loved you?"

She shook her head. His lips lowered to hers, and he kissed her with a hunger he hoped would show her a fraction of the depth of his feeling for her. When he ended the kiss, she lifted her lips to his and kissed him again. Nothing could've pleased him more.

Zach escorted his bride into her church to the whispers of several of his former neighbors. He'd forgotten that about small-town life. Everyone in Lake Bethel knew both of them, and when one person found out about the wedding, it would've spread through the congregation and the rest of the town in a nanosecond. He grinned down at his bride and laced his fingers through hers. Might as well let them see how in love they were so they could stop speculating. "Isn't that your sister?"

She visibly flinched. "Yes. That's her."

"Is that Ben she's with?"

"It is."

"I thought he moved back to Maryland when they divorced."

"They're not divorced."

"I thought they were."

"Separated."

"Oh."

"I guess we should sit with them." She made her way to their pew and slid in beside her sister. He followed suit.

"I didn't expect to see you here." Addison poked Parker in the ribs with her elbow.

Parker leaned close to her sister. "I guess what you said got to me, so I came to a Wednesday night meeting, and the pastor suggested I come again today."

"I hope you'll find what you're looking for." Addison glanced over at Ben and waved her fingers in his direction.

"What are you doing in Pennsylvania?"

"It's a long story that involves his crazy ex-girlfriend, so I don't think we have time to squeeze it in before the sermon. Come out to eat with us after, and I'll fill you in."

"Is it okay if Ben joins us?"

"He's welcome. He is still your husband, right?"

"Yeah. I guess so."

"Well, he's family, so he's welcome."

"Thanks." Parker gave Addison a brief hug before they were asked to open their hymnals and sing hymn number 350 "Tis' So Sweet to Trust in Jesus." He reveled in the sound of his wife and her sister's voices as he sang along with the rest of the congregation. The two would make a great duet, a soprano and an alto, both voices strong and clear. The words of the song called him to reflect, and once again he recognized his failure to trust in Him who gave him life.

The flight back to California was so much nicer than the commercial flight she'd taken to Philadelphia. She leaned against her husband and reveled in the feel of his muscular arm across her shoulders. When she nuzzled his neck, he groaned.

He leaned down to whisper in her ear. "You'd better stop that if you want me to behave myself."

Not wanting to push her luck, she eased up on her flirtations. It felt great to be free to show affection for him now. The weight of her secret had prevented her from expressing herself. Now, she felt unencumbered.

When they arrived back at the mansion, she practically skipped to the front door. A shot rang out before she could get inside. A glass panel inches from her head exploded. The driver dove on top of her to protect her from the next shot. Another man inside the house opened the door and drug her inside. Then the driver followed them inside and barked out orders. Several armed men ran outside and covered Zach so he could get inside safely.

"What's going on?" Her voice trembled as she searched Zach's eyes. "Who are these men?"

"They're our bodyguards."

"Why didn't you tell me you hired bodyguards?"

"I was hoping to be discreet about it, but after what happened to you and Javier, I thought a bodyguard was a safer option than a regular driver."

"I should say so. I think he saved my life."

"It seems he did. Let's go upstairs. They've already contacted the police, so we don't have long before we'll have to give our statements."

She heard another gunshot. "Someone is still out there shooting! Do you think it's Nikki?"

"Most likely." He rubbed his temples. "I don't think anyone else wants us dead."

They hurried upstairs to the master bedroom, and she tried to shake off the dread that was building in her stomach. When would this come to an end?

Alternating between pacing the floor and cuddling up under a blanket on the loveseat, she waited for the police to call her downstairs to give her statement. There wasn't much to tell them, so it didn't take long. Back upstairs, she clung to Zach, grateful that he hadn't been hurt. Hours had passed since the attempt on their lives, but every noise in the house made her jump.

Zach stared into her eyes. "I think we should go to a hotel for the night."

"I can't be afraid in our own house. I've got to get used to living here."

"No you don't. If you have trouble with it, we'll move."

"You're crazy."

"Crazy, yes. If that means I'd move anywhere for you." He packed a bag for her. "We will stay in a hotel tonight; I'll have Ames set something up. We need not decide tonight whether we want to move."

"Amy doesn't know about this."

"No. I imagine she doesn't." His brow furrowed. "She's not going to like it."

Amy grabbed Addison's arm. "Who's the hotty in the hallway, and why did I get the third degree before being allowed to see you?"

"The 'hotty' in the hallway is our bodyguard." Zach answered for her. "He saved my wife's life this evening."

"Saved your life? How?"

"Someone tried to shoot me. Or else they intentionally missed by inches. Who can know?"

"The nut who tried to shoot you would know. Did they get her? Was it Nikki?"

"Surprisingly, no." Addison let out a deep sigh. "She has an airtight alibi since she was in jail at the time of the shooting."

Amy crinkled up her nose. "No way."

"Yes way." Addison flopped down on the bed. "I'm sure she was involved, but we need to find the proof."

"I'd like to know how we're supposed to start a family with crazy people trying to shoot at us." Zach paced the floor.

"Whoa there, Zach. Take your time. You've only been married for two-weeks. Give the girl some breathing room."

Addison grinned. "He's fine. We both want to start a family."

"Really? Already? Don't you want to enjoy married life for a few months first?"

"We'll have nine months for that, right?"

"Wait. Are you pregnant?" Amy's eyebrows shot up. "Already?"

"No." Addison laughed. "I'm not pregnant."

"But you're trying?"

"Not yet, but soon."

"Not if we can't keep you safe."

"You have Garrison Securities handling it. I'm sure they'll work with the authorities and take care of everything."

"Are you sure you're the same girl who was in full panic mode less than two hours ago?"

"After the meeting with your security experts, I feel much better."

"I'm glad one of us does."

"Did you know I designed their website?"

"No. I did not know that." He shook his head. "Small world."

"My father would say 'try painting it.'"

"Your father was a trip."

"I miss him."

He put his arm around her shoulders. "I know you do."

Amy snapped her fingers. "Focus." She waved her arms in the air. "What's next?"

"What's next is you go home and get some sleep. Tomorrow morning you go into the office as usual, but Mr. Hotty out in the hallway will be there when you arrive and will follow you everywhere you go," Zach said.

"Does this bodyguard have a name?"

"Seamus."

"Don't you have a woman or a married man you can assign to me?"

"What makes you think Seamus isn't married?"

"Do you honestly think I didn't check out his ring finger on the way in here?"

"Some men don't wear wedding rings."

"True." She grinned. "Ask him for me, will you?"

"Not a chance." Zach plopped down on the bed beside Addison.

"I will," Addison piped up.

Zach narrowed his eyes.

"What? She needs to know." The corner of her mouth turned up in a crooked grin. "Especially if you're going to assign Mr. Hotty as her bodyguard."

"I didn't assign him, Grayson Garrison did." He flattened his lips into a hard line. "Maybe I should call Gray and get Seamus unassigned."

Addison sat up and placed her hand on his cheek. "Leave well enough alone."

He shook his head.

There was a knock on the door, and Seamus stuck his head in. "The police arrested the sniper, but he's not talking yet."

Zach watched as Seamus McPherson entered the conference room where they were all seated awaiting his update. "I've got some news."

"I should hope so, since you've called us out of an important meeting." Amy leaned back in her chair and crossed her legs.

The man made eye contact with Amy, completely ignoring him and Addison. "They found evidence that Nikki West hired the sniper to take your boss out." The bodyguard frowned. "The man is a homeless Army veteran." Seamus turned to face Zach. "She offered him twenty grand to kill you. That's twice the going rate."

Zach shook his head. "Wow. I knew it was the most likely scenario, but it's freaky thinking a woman I came close to marrying tried to have me killed."

Seamus kept steady eye contact. "The man claims to have missed Addison intentionally. He was willing to scare her, but murdering an innocent woman was out of his comfort zone. You, he would've killed if given the opportunity."

Zach rose to his feet. "Comforting." He held out his hand to Addison. "Want to get out of here and celebrate Nikki getting caught?"

Addison placed her hand in his. "Maybe now we can trust that she won't be granted bail."

"I should hope not." Zach nodded at Seamus and Amy and opened the door for Addison. "Where do you want to go to celebrate Ms. West's incarceration?"

"Home. Let's go home."

"I like the sound of that." He placed a kiss on top of her head and pushed the button for the elevator. "Tomorrow morning we'll fly out to our island. The tree house is finished, so we can have that real honeymoon we talked about." They got on the elevator.

"I'd love that." She stood on her tiptoes and kissed him with all the feeling she'd been holding back. "I think I'm ready for a real honeymoon with the man I love."

"That's what I was hoping to hear, love." He grinned.

Epilogue

One Year Later

Addison watched Zach take the sleeping infant from the crib. She'd finally gotten Amelia to sleep, but that didn't keep him from disturbing her.

He grinned when he noticed her watching from the doorway. "Caught again, huh?"

"It's a good thing you're cute. I don't think anyone else would get away with waking that child."

"I didn't wake her. She's still sleeping." He smiled down at the baby in his arms. "Are you happy, Addison?"

"Absolutely. I can't imagine being happier."

"Are you ready for more children?"

"Don't you want to give me time to recover from the first birth?"

"Do you still want a whole houseful of kids?"

She shrugged. "When did I say I wanted a houseful of children?"

"In 2006."

"And you remember that?" The corner of her mouth lifted.

"I plan to hold you to it." He kissed Amelia's head and lay her back in the crib. As soon as her head hit the mattress, she wailed.

"Oh, boy." Addison put her hands on her hips and glared at him. "I suppose you're off to work now?"

"You know it." He smiled. "I love you."

She shook her head. "I love you too, but you're in trouble for waking the baby."

"Sorry." He smiled sheepishly and scooted past her.

She lifted the newborn from her crib and cuddled her close, breathing in the smell of Baby Magic. She was grateful to God for the many blessings in her life, and when Zach returned home from work, it would be soon enough to tell him they were expecting their second child. There was no making up for the child he'd lost, and he'd have to live with that pain, but she'd gladly give him as many children as the Lord would bless them with.

DEAR READER,

I hope you enjoyed reading my novel, *The Billionaire's Reluctant Bride.* Please check out some of my other titles.

I'd love it if you'd sign up for my newsletter at https://www.elleekay.com/newsletter-sign-up/.

If you enjoyed *The Billionaire's Reluctant Bride*, the most helpful thing you can do is leave an honest review. So, please consider submitting a review on Amazon and/or GoodReads. It costs nothing other than a moment of your time and can be tremendously beneficial. Your quick review helps to get my book into the hands of other readers who may enjoy it.

https://www.amazon.com/
https://www.goodreads.com/

For a list of my current books and upcoming releases check out the novel page on my website: https://www.elleekay.com/novels/

Thank you.
Elle E. Kay
https://www.elleekay.com

About Elle E. Kay

Elle E. Kay lives in Central Pennsylvania. She loves life in the country on her hobby farm with her husband, Joe. Elle is a born-again Christian with a deep faith and love for the Lord Jesus Christ. She desires to live for Him and to put Him first in everything she does.

She writes children's books under the pen-name Ellie Mae Kay.

You can connect with Elle on her website and blog at https://www.elleekay.com/ or on social media:

Facebook: https://www.facebook.com/ElleEKay7
Twitter: https://twitter.com/ElleEKay7
Pinterest: https://www.pinterest.com/elleekay7/
Amazon Author Central: http://www.amazon.com/author/ellekay
Instagram: https://www.instagram.com/elleekay7/
Goodreads: https://www.goodreads.com/author/show/15016833.Elle_E_Kay

I'd love it if you'd sign up for my newsletter at https://www.elleekay.com/newsletter-sign-up/.

ACKNOWLEDGEMENTS

I would like to give special thanks to my husband, Joe, for putting up with the long hours of writing and editing.

This story is a product of my imagination and a work of fiction. Names, characters, businesses, places, events, locales, and incidents are either the products of my imagination or in the case of actual towns, historical persons, and companies mentioned, they have been used in a fictitious manner. Any resemblance to actual persons, living or dead, or actual events is purely coincidental.

Any errors or deficiencies are my own.

PERSONAL TESTIMONY

I first came to know Jesus as a young teen, but before long I strayed from God and allowed my selfish desires to rule me. I sought after acceptance and love from my peers, not knowing that only God could fill my emptiness. My teen years were full of angst and misery, for me and my family. People I loved were hurt by my selfishness. My heartache was at times overwhelming, but I couldn't find the healing I desperately desired. After several runaway attempts my family was left with little choice, and they put me in a group home/residential facility where I would get the constant supervision I needed.

At that home I met a godly man called 'Big John' who tried once again to draw me back to Jesus. He would point out Matthew 11:28-30 and remind me that all I had to do to find peace was give my cares to Christ. I wanted to live a Christian life, but something kept pulling me away. The cycle continued well into adulthood. I would call out to God, but then I would turn away from Him. (If you read the old testament, you'll see that the nation of Israel had a similar pattern, they would call out to God and He would heal them and bring them back into their land. Then they would stray, and He would chastise them. It was a cycle that went on and on).

When I came to realize that God's love was still available to me despite all my failings, I found peace and joy that have remained with me to do this day. It wasn't God who kept walking away. He'd placed his seal on me in childhood and no matter how far I ran from Him, **He remained faithful.** When I finally recognized His unfailing love, I was made free.

2 Timothy 2:13
"If we believe not, yet he abideth faithful: he cannot deny himself."
Ephesians 4:30
"And grieve not the holy Spirit of God, whereby ye are sealed unto the day of redemption."

I let myself be drawn into His loving arms and led by His precious nail-scarred hands. He has kept me securely at His side and taught me important life lessons. Jesus has given me back the freedom I had in Christ on that day when I accepted the precious gift He'd offered. My life in Him is so much fuller than it ever was when I tried to live by the world's standards.

I implore you, if you've known Jesus and strayed, call out to Him.

If you've never known Jesus Christ as your personal Lord and Saviour. Find out what it means to have a relationship with Christ. Not religion, but a personal relationship with a loving God.

God makes it clear in His word that there isn't a person righteous enough to get to heaven on their own.

Romans 3:10
"As it is written, There is none righteous, no, not one:"

We are all sinners.

Romans 3:23
For all have sinned, and come short of the glory of God;

Death is the penalty for sin.

Romans 6:23

"For the wages of sin is death; but the gift of God is eternal life through Jesus Christ our Lord."

Christ died on the cross for our sins.

Romans 5:8
"But God commendeth his love toward us, in that, while we were yet sinners, Christ died for us."

If we confess and believe we will be saved.

Romans 10:9
"That if thou shalt confess with thy mouth the Lord Jesus, and shalt believe in thine heart that God hath raised him from the dead, thou shalt be saved."

Once we believe he sets us free.

Romans 8:1
"There is therefore now no condemnation to them which are in Christ Jesus, who walk not after the flesh, but after the Spirit."

I hope you'll take hold of that freedom and start a personal relationship with Christ Jesus.

Made in the USA
Columbia, SC
08 April 2021